# Out of the Ordinary

## by Michelle M. Barone

*Boxcar houses, typical of the one Julia's family occupied.*

## Adventures in History

History Compass, LLC
Boston, Massachusetts

*Zadie — Have fun reading this book. Enjoy this Colorado story. Warm Wishes*
*2013*

# HistoryCompass
www.historycompass.com

© 2005 Michelle M. Barone

2nd edition

ISBN 1-932663-10-X


10 9 8 7 6 5 4 3 2 1


*Printed in Canada*


Subjet Reference Guide
Barone, Michelle M.
Out of the Ordinary / Michelle Barone.
United States - Colorado mining town life -
one - room schoolhouse - Ludlow Massacre.

## Summary

Historical fiction. Young Julia lives in the mining town of Phippsburg, Colorado in the early 20th century. She wishes for something out of the ordinary to happen in her very predictable life. When she finds out about an impending mine disaster, her whole world changes.

Based on the life of Julia Iannacito.

# ✛ Dedication ✛

This book is dedicated to my grandmother,
Julia Iannacito Barone, who gave me her love, her
wisdom, and her story, and to my daughter, Alex, who,
like my grandmother, came here from a far away land.

# Table of Contents

The Crime ..................................................................7

The Punishment ........................................................ 11

The Daydream .......................................................... 14

The Hero .................................................................. 19

The Journey ............................................................. 25

The Writing Lesson .................................................. 29

The Job .................................................................... 33

The Hiding Place ...................................................... 36

The Store ................................................................. 39

The Headlines .......................................................... 42

The Spy .................................................................... 47

The Plan ................................................................... 51

The Note .................................................................. 57

The Delivery ............................................................ 60

The Chosen One ....................................................... 64

The Disguise ............................................................ 69

Lost and Found ........................................................ 74

Adventure ................................................................ 76

The Thing................................................................. 79

The Red Sweater ...................................................... 81

The Bell Ringer ................................................................ 85

The Apology ................................................................... 87

The Interpreter ............................................................... 89

The Revelation ................................................................ 92

The Miners .................................................................... 95

The Wish ...................................................................... 98

The Visit ..................................................................... 100

The Boxcar House ............................................................. 102

The History behind the Story ................................................. 105

    Family History ........................................................... 106

    The Ludlow Massacre ...................................................... 109

    Going to School in a One-Room Schoolhouse ............. 113
        *Vanishing One-Room Rural Schools* by Leo VanMeer

    Letter from a Former Student and Teacher of
    One-Room Schoolhouses ............................................. 116
        by Mrs. Reppie Smith

    Photographs and Artifacts ................................................ 118

Acknowledgments ............................................................. 120

# The Crime

Wishing is free. It doesn't cost anything. It doesn't cost money anyway.

Mama says wishing costs you being happy in the moment. She says wishing costs you being happy with what you've got.

Julia figured it wasn't wishing's fault if people weren't happy. Julia wasn't unhappy. Wishing made her happier.

Julia Iannacito's head was full of wishes. Wishing made the long school day shorter. It made the cold walk home warmer. It made everything sweeter. It made ordinary things special.

Wishing was magic. It could take Julia anywhere, anytime. It could give her anything. Mama said wishing was dangerous. Julia knew that coal mining was dangerous, but not wishing. What could be dangerous about wishing?

Julia sat in her assigned seat in the fifth grade. She looked at her *McGuffey Reader* and wished that school weren't so boring.

'Woosh! Splat!' A gooshy, white spitball whizzed past Julia's ear. It smushed onto the blackboard and stuck. Julia watched a wet stream travel down from the wad. It left a shiny black trail on the board. There was only one person in the room who would do such a thing. Julia knew who it was.

Julia knew what would happen next. It was the same thing that happened every time Teddy Parker misbehaved.

Miss Crawford, the teacher, spun around and faced the class like a fighter squaring off against an opponent. "Who made this spitball?" she demanded.

Julia clamped her skinny legs together and froze in her seat. Her knobby knees bumped each other.

"Who made this spitball?" Miss Crawford repeated.

"It wasn't any of the sixth graders," said Frank O'Malley, a blond haired, Irish boy. He stood, as was the custom, to speak for his age group.

Julia knew she was expected to answer. She was the only fifth grader in the room who spoke English. The other fifth grade girl sat wide-eyed with sealed lips.

Julia wished they didn't have to go through this ritual every time Teddy Parker acted up. Teddy's family came to Phippsburg long before Julia's. Teddy lived in a real house. Julia's family lived in an old boxcar that had been taken off of the rails. There were other families from Italy, Ireland, and Greece living in the boxcar section of town.

Julia didn't know why Teddy was a troublemaker. He was luckier than all of the other kids. Teddy's father ran the coal mine where everyone else's father worked.

"The fourth graders didn't do it," said a girl popping up and down in one motion.

Julia had missed her turn to answer.

"It wasn't any of the third graders, Miss Crawford," said another girl.

"The second graders didn't do it," said Teddy's sister, Paulina.

A small boy stood. "It wasn't the first grade, Teacher," he said.

"There will be a punishment for this," Miss Crawford said. "Whoever made this spitball will have to come to the front of the room."

Julia watched Miss Crawford focus on Teddy. He shifted in his wooden seat at the end of the sixth grade row.

"What do you have to say, Teddy?" asked Miss Crawford.

Julia looked at Teddy sitting in his new clothes from Denver. He wore a new shirt under a new sweater, new knickers, and new knee socks. Julia guessed his underwear was new, too. Teddy's clothes were the right size, not patched and baggy hand-me-downs like Julia's. Most of the kids were dressed like her, in clothes that had once been worn by their parents.

Julia watched Teddy slowly rise. He stepped out to the side of his desk. Julia waited for Teddy to make his confession. It was his chance to show off every day. She knew in a moment he would proudly walk to the front of the room, stand on tip toe, and place his nose on a chalk dot Miss Crawford drew on the board. The class would watch him stand there on pointed toe while he took his punishment. Miss Crawford wouldn't make Teddy stand at the board for a whole hour like she would any other student. Teddy was her pet. She'd call off his punishment after five or ten minutes.

It was the same every time. Nothing exciting ever happened in Phippsburg. Why couldn't it be a little bit different this once?

Julia reached up and felt a rag curl in her hair. Mama tied the rags into her hair last night. Julia liked how the curls made a soft half circle around her plain face.

Julia closed her eyes and made one silent wish. "Please let something exciting happen today for a change."

She opened her eyes and blinked three times for good luck.

Miss Crawford was waiting for an answer. Teddy straightened his shoulders and drew in a long, deep breath.

"Miss Crawford, I must tell the truth," he said.

"Yes, you must," said Miss Crawford.

All eyes were glued on Teddy Parker.

"It was…Julia Iannacito!" he announced.

# The Punishment

"What?" said Julia. She couldn't stop herself from gasping.

"It was Julia. I saw her," said Teddy.

It was then that a second shocking thing occurred.

"I saw it, too," said Paulina Parker.

"Are you sure, Paulina?" asked Miss Crawford.

"Yes, Ma'am," said Paulina without blinking.

Julia knew her mouth was hanging open as wide as her eyes.

"I…" she started to say something, but nothing came out.

"Did anyone else see what happened? Are there any other witnesses besides Paulina?" asked Miss Crawford.

Julia looked at the faces of her classmates. No one would meet her eyes. No one moved. No one spoke. Julia knew they wouldn't.

Since Teddy and Paulina's father was the boss at the coal mine, the other students worried that their fathers would suffer in some way or be fired if they spoke out against Teddy or Paulina Parker. Frank O'Malley shrugged and shook his head once when Julia glanced at him.

Miss Crawford's forehead crinkled for a moment before she said, "Step forward, Julia."

Children obeyed adults. Arguing was not allowed. The other fifth grader stared at Julia. The girl didn't understand what was happening.

"I'm coming," said Julia, like she was about to jump into a freezing river.

Julia did not look at Teddy as she walked past him. She had a father to protect, too.

Julia pictured Papa's scrubbed face as he sat at the table in the middle of their boxcar. She saw him in his red, woolen sweater eating hard bread for breakfast. He drank coffee as dark as the early mountain mornings. Before he left for the mines, he kissed Julia lightly on each eye. His coffee-warmed lips made her giggle.

Papa would say, "Do your best at school, Julia. You learn to read and write for Mama and me. We could never go to school in Italy. You do as the teacher says."

"Always, Papa," Julia would say.

Yes, Julia would do anything to protect her father. She pictured Papa walking into their boxcar at the end of the day. His clothes were blackened by coal dust. His eyes seemed so big in his charcoaled face. Papa was strict. No one misbehaved in Julia's family. She shuddered to think what Papa would say if he found out that she was in trouble at school.

"Step up to the board, Julia," said Miss Crawford. "Stand on your toes and put your nose right here."

Julia studied the lines on Miss Crawford's hand as she colored a chalk dot on the board. Julia had never been this close to Miss Crawford or her hands before. The teacher smelled like soap. Papa was the only one in Julia's family who got to clean up every night.

"I have to wash the layer of coal off once a day. It's enough to burn in the stove and heat our house for an hour," he would say.

Julia focused on the marble-sized chalk circle. She wondered if Miss Crawford bathed during the week instead of on Saturdays like everyone in Julia's family. Julia thought about how Mama heated water and washed Julia's younger sisters first. Then it was Julia's turn to use the same water in the silver, galvanized tub. Mama went next. Finally, Papa bathed in the water that had washed his family. Julia guessed Miss Crawford didn't have to share her bath water.

Julia stepped close to the chalkboard. She stood on tip toe.

"Teacher," squeaked a voice from the back of the room.

# The Daydream

J ulia rolled down from her toes. She turned around to see who was brave enough to say something.

"Speak up," said Miss Crawford.

There was no sound. Seconds ticked by silently. Whoever called out had changed his mind.

"Go on, Julia," said Miss Crawford.

It wasn't right, but Julia knew that some things in her world weren't fair no matter how she looked at them. Julia got back up on her toes and touched her nose to the cold, hard surface of the chalkboard.

"I'll tell you when your hour is up," said Miss Crawford. "You have plenty of time to stand there and think about what you've done!"

Julia's mind drifted. She thought about the yellow house with white curtains. It was where Teddy and Paulina Parker lived.

Chalk dust tickled her nose. "Aaaachoo!" Julia sneezed.

Someone giggled.

"Quiet!" barked Miss Crawford. "Get out your tablets. It's time for arithmetic."

Julia kept her nose on the chalk dot. She guessed two minutes had gone by. She strained her eyes to look sideways at the marks Miss Crawford made on the board.

"First graders, add these numbers," said Miss Crawford.

Julia saw little puffs of white dust coming off of the chalk as Miss Crawford wrote. Clicking echoed in Julia's ears. The chalk made only light ticks on the board from her seat in the fifth grade row.

Julia closed her eyes and imagined Mama cooking in the yellow house. She wished her family lived there. Papa said wishes are like fishes. They swim away before you can catch them, before they can do you any good. But Julia caught one right now, and she held on. Things would be different if she lived in a real house like the Parkers.

She pictured Angela and Lucia playing in the yard. She saw herself running to greet Papa as he came through the front gate. He was dressed in a white shirt. There was not a speck of coal dust on him.

Miss Crawford's voice brought Julia back to the schoolhouse for a moment.

"Second and third graders will do these subtraction problems," said Miss Crawford. "Fourth graders, work on these multiplication problems."

Julia closed her eyes. She had plenty of time for wishing now. She was joined by her sisters in her mind as they pulled Papa into the yellow house.

"Dinner will be ready soon," said Mama.

"The children and I will play while we wait," said Papa.

This was the life Julia longed for – in a house, not in a boxcar. She wanted a real house like Teddy and Paulina's.

It was after school on Friday afternoons when Julia delivered the Parkers' clean laundry and picked up their dirty clothes. Mama washed the Parkers' clothes to earn extra money.

"It's to buy food," Mama told Julia in Italian.

Julia watched Mama put the coins into an empty coffee can. Julia kept track. Mama never spent the money on food. Julia hoped she was saving up so they could live in a real house someday.

Miss Crawford's voice cut through Julia's thoughts. From her spot on the chalkboard Julia heard, "Fifth graders, do these long division problems."

Math was Julia's favorite subject. It seemed like a double punishment to stand here with her nose stuck on the board and have to miss working the problems.

"Sixth graders, work on these fractions." Miss Crawford stood close to Julia now. Julia could easily see $4/5 + 1/10$.

Ten is the common denominator, thought Julia. She liked numbers. They were neat and fit a pattern. Julia had a feel for how they worked, and right answers were automatic for her. Thinking about numbers reminded her of last week when Mrs. Parker paid her for the laundry.

"Tell your mother that the stitching around this shirt cuff is superb. You Italians can really sew. I love the way she mends our clothes," said Mrs. Parker.

"I'll tell her," said Julia. Mama didn't know how to sew. Julia had stayed up the night before finishing the last stitches by the light of an oil lamp. She listened to her parents breathing in their bed on one side of the boxcar and her sisters on the other. She was glad that Angela and

16

Lucia had warmed up the box bed by the time she crawled in and fell asleep.

"Julia, do something for me while you're here," said Mrs. Parker.

"Yes, Ma'am," said Julia.

"Work a few multiplication problems with Teddy. I think a little practice with a classmate will help him," said Mrs. Parker.

"I don't need help!" said Teddy, coming into the kitchen.

"You can do a few problems right here at the table," said Mrs. Parker as if she hadn't heard her son. "You two can have some cookies and milk while you work."

Julia stared at the cookies and milk. She saw minute grains of sugar shining like snow flakes on the cookies. Julia imagined taking a bite. Her mouth watered.

"It's easy, Teddy," said Julia. "If you have four times three, you can imagine four plates with three cookies on each one. If you count the cookies, you'll see that four times three is twelve in all."

"I said I don't need help!" Teddy stomped out the back door.

Julia figured eating cookies wasn't special for Teddy. She figured he could eat them any time he wanted to. She figured it was easy for Teddy Parker to walk away from multiplication and cookies in the same moment.

"I didn't want you to make him mad," said Mrs. Parker. "You'd better go. Give the money to your mother."

"Yes, Mrs. Parker," said Julia. She put her hand in her pocket to make sure the coins were still there. Julia walked home thinking of the uneaten cookies on the table. She wondered if she ever would taste such a thing. Mama fixed dinner every night, but there was never money for dessert or anything else like cookies.

A chill in the one room schoolhouse brought Julia's attention back to the present moment. Her eyes crossed as she focused on the dot under the tip of her nose. I guess Teddy's getting me back for showing him up at math, thought Julia.

"Class, prepare to recite your answers," said Miss Crawford.

Julia knew Teddy wouldn't have his answers ready. He'd make some excuse like he did every day. Teddy always got treated special.

I'd like to be special like Teddy just once, thought Julia.

"Time's up, Julia!" Miss Crawford's voice rang out.

Julia got off her tip toes. Her feet tingled from standing in one position too long.

Julia wasn't sure she could walk properly. She put her hands on the icy chalkboard to steady herself. When she dropped her hands, Julia was horrified to see the dark spots her sweaty fingertips left on the blackboard. A fine layer of perspiration formed on Julia's forehead. Normally she would welcome the warmth inside of her but not now. Julia wiped the spots on the board furiously with the sleeve of her blouse. Satisfied, she turned away from the board and faced the class. Everyone stared at her.

The silence hurt Julia's ears.

# The Hero

J ulia pulled on her ears. Silence remained the loudest thing in the room.

Julia noticed a girl in the front row. The curly haired first grader was rubbing the tip of her nose. Julia touched her nose with her right hand. She saw chalk dust on her fingertips. Julia wiped the point of her nose on her sleeve to remove the rest of the white powder. She nodded once at the first grader to thank her.

Julia's footsteps sounded like a drum as she walked back to her seat. Most of her classmates looked down at their paper tablets. Teddy stared at her with a bold grin pasted across his face. He looked like he'd just caught the biggest fish anyone had ever seen. Julia fixed her eyes on the fifth grade row and focused on her own seat. It pulled her with a gravitational force. Julia slid onto the cold, hard chair. She quickly wrote the math problems for her grade.

'Smack!'

Julia looked up to see Teddy's tablet hit the floor.

"My answers are smudged!" said Teddy. "I can't read them Miss Crawford!"

Julia knew that whether they were smudged or not, Teddy's answers wouldn't do him much good. Miss Crawford checked her watch.

"It's time to ring the bell, anyway. Teddy would you ring it please?" she asked.

It seems like Miss Crawford works at the mine under Teddy's father, too, thought Julia. It's as if we all work for the Parkers one way or another.

Teddy rang the bell as everyone buttoned up their heavy coats. Although it was April, winter had a hold on Colorado and wasn't letting go. Julia wrapped Mama's old black coat around her own thin frame. The long sleeves hanging way over her hands were the only gloves she'd ever had.

Teddy finished ringing the school bell. He pushed ahead of everyone to be the first one out of the door. His new, blue coat flapped open at his sides. He looked like a goose fanning its wings as he ran. Julia watched him disappear around the corner of the school.

Frank O'Malley, the oldest boy in the class, came up to Julia outside. He tucked his wheat colored hair under his cap.

"It was wrong what Teddy and Paulina did to you today," he said. "You know no one could stand up for you."

"I know," said Julia. "It's just the way it is here."

"Everyone's afraid we'll get kicked out of our homes like the miners' families in Ludlow if we stand up against a Parker," the boy said.

Julia recognized the name, Ludlow. "Papa told me about Ludlow. It sounds terrible. No one can say a word against Teddy, Paulina, or the mine because of it."

"Sh-sh, keep your voice down. The miners and their families are sleeping outside in tents. None of us would survive living in tents in these mountains." He pulled his hat down over his reddening ears. "My father says it's warmer in southern Colorado than it is here in Phippsburg. It's the only reason the Ludlow families are surviving outside. They're having trouble because the miners asked for better working conditions. When the mine owners wouldn't help them, the miners went on strike."

"Is that when they got kicked out of their homes?" asked Julia.

"Yeah, the mine owners put them and their wives and children outside in the cold," said Frank.

Julia imagined her family living outside in a tent. They'd freeze to death the first night.

"I guess it really makes the mine owners angry when miners ask for anything," said Julia.

"You've got it," said Frank. "Some rich family called the Rockefellers owns the mines near Ludlow. My father says as long as they're comfortable and making lots of money they don't care what happens to the miners who are cutting the coal. The Rockefellers are powerful. A strike is the only way the miners can stand up for themselves."

"Who will win?" asked Julia.

"Nobody knows," said Frank, motioning for Julia to walk with him on the road leading away from the school. "We don't want anyone to hear us." He lowered his voice to a hoarse whisper. Julia strained her ears to make out what Frank was saying. "At least the Ludlow miners are trying. Our fathers do whatever Boss Parker tells them. I heard some miners talking with my dad. They said something about union men passing as miners here in Phippsburg to work on the inside. They want Mr. Parker to pay our fathers more money and to make eight hour shifts instead of twelve. Someone told my father there's a law in Colorado about eight hours being the right amount for workers."

"Are you saying Mr. Parker is breaking the law?" asked Julia.

"Sure, all of the mine owners are," said Frank. "There's more, too. The union wants miners to get paid for all of their work, like when they lay rails or clean up timber. It's not right that they do all kinds of work at the mine but only get paid for digging coal."

"It doesn't seem right," said Julia.

"My father says the union also wants to make it so miners can shop at any store, not just the mine-owned store where the prices are high. Miners should be able to live wherever they want instead of in the mine-owned housing," said Frank.

"Mr. Parker lets us live in one of the boxcars on the other side of the Yampa River," said Julia.

"We live in one of Mr. Parker's wooden storage shacks. There's a bunch of them for miners on the other side of the railroad tracks," explained Frank.

"Is it true? Are there union workers in our mine here?" asked Julia.

"Maybe there are," said Frank. "I know you won't say a word about this, Julia."

"I promise. Papa is thankful for his job at the mine. I don't want any trouble for him," said Julia.

"My father says it's hard and dangerous, but mining

is the only work here for an immigrant. Maybe something will happen here if union workers can sneak into the mine. Anyway, if the protesting miners and their union win in Ludlow, it will help all Colorado miners," he said.

"Will it make Teddy Parker nicer?" asked Julia.

"Probably not, but he wouldn't be able to bully us all so much," said Frank.

"Maybe the union would make things better for our fathers," said Julia.

"Sure it would. Anyway, it wasn't fair what Teddy did to you. You were strong today, Julia!"

"It wouldn't have done any good to argue with Teddy and Paulina. Miss Crawford has to treat them special. Mr. Parker pays her, too. I'd better get going. I'll see you tomorrow," said Julia, turning to head for home.

As she walked alone, she thought about her wish for something different to happen today.

I guess taking Teddy's punishment was different. What a silly wish! I wish I could help the union somehow, but how can children help? A girl could never help! Girls aren't allowed anywhere near a mine.

Teddy Parker's face appeared in Julia's mind. If Papa ran the mine, I don't think it would make me treat people mean, thought Julia.

Julia wondered if it would make her feel better if she treated Teddy just a little bit mean. The idea turned her insides as cold as her wet feet trudging through the Rocky Mountain snow.

Julia's right foot hit a patch of ice and slid out from under her. She fell straight down and bounced on her bottom. She heard giggling in the Aspen grove behind her. Julia scrambled to her feet and spun around. She strained her eyes to see who was hiding in the trees. Julia heard snow crunching under clumsy feet, too heavy to belong to a deer.

"Who's there?" she called, not expecting an answer. "Who is it?"

Julia listened to the feet getting softer as they moved further away.

Who's following me? she wondered. Did they hear me talking to Frank about Ludlow and the mine?

Julia scanned the trees. She saw something for a fraction of a second, but it was long enough.

# The Journey

A flash of blue sped from Julia's eyes to her brain and registered recognition. Her blood ran like an icy river through her. Had Teddy been able to hear her conversation about the mine? Julia hoped she and Frank had kept their voices low enough, but she couldn't be sure. The thought of Teddy Parker knowing what she had said made her stomach flip. Julia shook her head to erase the image of Teddy running away through the trees.

Julia walked home along the Yampa River. Sometimes the river ran black from the miners dumping in the water they used to wash off coal. This afternoon it looked like a picture the way the brush shone rusted red, burnt orange and yellow-gold along the banks above the white snow. Julia crossed the railroad tracks. She picked up a few stray lumps of coal that had fallen from the train cars as they bumped along. Julia stuffed the coal into her coat pockets. She plodded the rest of the way home.

Julia slid open the door to the boxcar. Heat from the coal stove in the center of the rectangle-shaped room hit her face.

"Julia!" squealed Angela.

"Shhh!" said Mama, putting her finger to her lips. "Lucia's still napping."

Julia peeked at her little sister asleep on the corner box bed the children shared. She was snuggled under the patched blanket that Julia had sewn from scraps of old clothing and then stuffed with rags.

Julia took the coal from her pockets and added it to the heap in the bucket next to the stove. She took off her sopping shoes and adjusted the water-logged square of material she kept tucked inside her left shoe to plug a hole. Her feet stung as they thawed by the stove.

"Wash your hands and help us," said Mama.

Julia swished her hands in a bowl of cold water and dried them on a rough towel. She picked up a knife and cut the macaroni dough that Mama had already rolled out flat.

"Tell us a story, Mama," pleaded Angela.

"Tell us about coming to America," said Julia.

"You've heard that story a hundred times," said Mama.

"Tell it a hundred and one times then," said Julia. "We had an adventure. It was exciting."

"You are always wishing for adventure and excitement, Julia. Coming here was enough adventure for me," said Mama.

"Please tell the story. It will make our work go faster," said Julia.

"You know your Papa came to America to work on the railroad. Someone he met got him a job working in the coal mines instead. Papa sent for me to join him. I told him to send enough money for two. Julia, you had been born and Papa hadn't even seen you yet."

"We still lived with Grandma in Abruzzo back then," said Julia.

"That's right," said Mama. "I sent your picture to Papa. He slept with it under his pillow every night until he could see you. It took Papa two years to earn enough money to send for us. Finally, we got on a ship and said goodbye to Italy forever."

"Was it so bad in Italy?" asked Angela.

"We were very poor, Angela. In America we have a chance to do better. We have a home. We are lucky here," said Mama.

Julia spread a handful of damp noodles on the table to dry.

"We are lucky here," Julia repeated. She thought of the yellow house again.

"Tell about the ship, Mama," Julia said, pushing the yellow house out of her mind.

Mama took a big breath. "We were on the ship for twenty-one days. One night there was a terrible storm. The waves bounced the ship like a rubber ball. Everyone got sick. I took you, Julia, up to the deck to get some air. Suddenly a giant wave tipped the boat! We started sliding to the side!"

"Eeeee!" squealed Angela.

"I couldn't hang on. We were being washed overboard!" said Mama.

Julia wasn't breathing. She always held her breath at this part of the story. She remembered slipping and sliding.

"I held your hand so tight, Mama," she whispered.

"I held yours too, and I prayed, 'Please God save us!'"

Then what happened, Mama?" Lucia asked from the bed.

"From nowhere a hand reached out and grabbed my coat," said Mama.

"It was the same coat that I wear to school," said Julia.

"A man, or an angel, grabbed the same coat. He pulled us back. I never saw his face. We were saved. When we got to America, we passed through Ellis Island. We rode the train to Colorado, to the mountains of Phippsburg, and to our new home in this boxcar."

Julia remembered being on the ship and how hopeful and fresh Mama's face looked back then. She stared at Mama's tired face across the table now. Julia wondered if Mama ever longed for something out of the ordinary to happen. Does Mama have a secret wish like I do?

"We are so lucky," said Angela, pinching a bead of dough.

Julia pictured Teddy and Paulina in the yellow house with the white curtains. She thought of the round sugar cookies. She remembered her nose on the chalk dot at school today. Julia couldn't hold back the slow sigh that deflated her lungs and her hopes.

"Yes, Angela. We are so lucky," said Julia.

# The Writing Lesson

"We are lucky to have money for flour, eggs, and milk," said Mama. "Julia, please go to the store and get some milk for your sisters' dinner. We need two more cans of tomatoes for sauce, and a piece of ham for Papa's breakfast tomorrow."

"Yes, Mama."

"I want to go too," pleaded Angela.

"You stay. It's too cold for you. Julia has my old coat," said Mama.

Julia took the coins Mama gave her. She noticed that Mama did not get them from her coffee can bank.

Outside, Julia saw her breath in the air. She walked on the dirt road toward the small Phippsburg Grocery Store. She slowed down going past the Parkers' yellow house.

I bet interesting things would happen to us if we lived there, thought Julia. We would really be lucky in the yellow house.

At that moment Teddy came out of the front door carrying a bundle of letters.

"Hey Julia, what's one spitball plus one spitball?" he asked.

29

"I think you know the answer to that," said Julia.

"I might need your help to figure it out," said Teddy, snickering. "Do you have a lot of letters to mail today?"

Julia could hardly stand being polite to Teddy. She imagined the things she might say if his father didn't run the mine.

"Not too many," said Julia. "I have to go to the store for Mama now, Teddy."

Julia's family never wrote letters to anyone. They never got letters from anyone, either. Even if they did get a letter, Mama and Papa couldn't read it.

Julia thought back a few months ago when Papa brought a paper home from the mines. Julia knew he didn't like having to ask Julia to read for him.

"You're the one who goes to school, Julia. Show me how you read," said Papa.

"It says, Notice to the workers of the Phippsburg Coal Mine: Day shifts are 6:00 A.M. to 6:00 P.M.," read Julia.

"I already know that," said Papa. "Twelve hours every day, seven days a week I work. I am lucky to have such a good job. Mr. Parker lets us live here in this nice boxcar."

"Will we ever live in a house like the Parkers?" asked Julia.

"Never complain about our house!" ordered Papa. "It's dangerous for a coal miner to complain. I could be fired!"

"Why, Papa?" asked Julia.

"There are bad things happening to miners in other parts of Colorado. A new miner told me about a place called Ludlow where miners tried to change things. It's coming to no good. The governor called in the National Guard to help keep the peace. I heard that the guard switched over and is

30

now working for the mine owners instead of the government. The mine owners are using the National Guard troops to protect their mines against union workers. It's illegal, but they're doing it. The Phippsburg mine is a nice mine. We don't have guards here and we don't want them! The guards are starting to shoot at miners in Ludlow."

"Where's Ludlow?" asked Julia.

"It's in the south part of Colorado by a place called Trinidad. I hear it's near the Colorado & Southern Railroad and west of the Denver & Rio Grande Railroad. It's far away from the mountains of Phippsburg, and it's a good thing, too! They've got that union trying to help the miners. Instead of helping them, it's hurting them! The miners got fired for joining that union, and their families lost their homes," said Papa.

"Will they ever get their homes back?" asked Julia.

"I don't know. It's enough questions. Never say a bad word about our home or the mines. I forbid it!" said Papa staring hard at his daughter.

"Yes, Papa," promised Julia. She was relieved to change the subject and get back to reading.

"There's more on this paper from the mine. It says night shifts are 6:00 P.M. to 6:00 A.M. You get paid $1.65 a day for either shift. Circle your shift and sign your name."

"You circle the day shift for me," said Papa.

Julia drew a circle around the day shift.

Papa stared at the paper for a few minutes. Then he said, "Show me how to write my name."

Julia moved closer to her father. The sleeve of his red woolen sweater felt scratchy against her arm. Papa smelled like soap, sweat, and the coal mine.

Papa gripped the pencil between coal-blackened fingers. Julia put her small hand on top of her father's large, rough one.

"Draw a line. From the top, draw a slant down and a slant up. Draw another line down. There's the M," said Julia.

"Keep going," said Papa.

"I is easy. Draw a straight line down."

Julia saw Papa's hand tremble. The I was wiggly.

"Draw another line. I'll help with the two slanted lines for the K. Now draw another line down. Make a line out of the top, the middle, and the bottom. There's your E. You're done with MIKE. Now we'll write Iannacito."

"It's too long. Make it shorter," said Papa.

"It's our name. How do I make it shorter?" asked Julia.

"I only want to write the end of it," said Papa. "I will write CITO."

"Yes Papa," said Julia, guiding his hand for a capital C, the i, the t, and the o.

"I am done with this paper. I am done with writing, and I have a new name, MIKE CITO."

Julia watched her father fold the paper and put it in his pocket. Julia Iannacito's papa had just become Mike Cito in one writing lesson. Julia suspected then that her father would never learn to read or write anything more than the two words in his name.

"Julia," said Teddy.

Teddy Parker's voice instantly snapped Julia back to the present. Julia stared at the stack of letters in Teddy's hand.

"Hey, Julia, I want you to do something for me," said Teddy.

# The Job

"You want me to do something for you, Teddy," said Julia. She felt prickling on the back of her neck. She figured it must be what a dog feels when the hair along its back stands straight up. Her senses sharpened as she braced herself for a trick.

"I want you to get these letters to the store so they'll get sent out with the mail. Since you're going to the store anyway, you could deliver them. You might as well be the only one getting chilled. My father says you European peasants are like animals. You can take the weather better than us. It really is getting too cold for me to be outside," said Teddy.

Julia stared at Teddy's warm, blue coat, the same blue coat that had flapped open after school, the same blue coat that she saw racing away through the trees, the same blue coat that was surely warmer than Mama's tattered coat she now wore. Teddy's words about European peasants being like animals was finding a permanent place to stick in Julia's memory.

"I see you're thinking about it. You drive a hard bargain, Julia," said Teddy digging in his pocket. He pulled out a dime and dropped it into Julia's coat pocket.

33

"Now I've paid you for the job," said Teddy. He tossed the letters at Julia and ran into the warm, yellow house.

Julia reached in her pocket and felt the dime. I can put this in Mama's can for a real house someday, thought Julia. Every little bit helps.

Julia didn't really want to do anything for Teddy Parker, but he had paid her, and there were letters laying on top of the frozen snow. Julia stooped down and gathered the envelopes. She noticed a piece of paper folded in half. It was not inside an envelope. Julia didn't mean to see it, but she saw it. The word Ludlow jumped out at her from the middle of some writing on the paper. Julia put the note on top of the letters and turned her back to the yellow house. She started walking in the direction of the store again.

Julia knew it was wrong to read other people's mail, but this was an open note. Julia had seen the word, "Ludlow." What if it's about the miners in Ludlow? What if it's about the union and our mine in Phippsburg? What if I can help Papa somehow, thought Julia. She looked back to make sure Teddy wasn't behind her or watching her through a window. Convinced that she was alone, Julia walked slowly as she unfolded the note. She read:

> Evans,
>
> I have identified the union spies. I know they are in our mine. I heard some of our men talking with those new miners we hired. The new men are from Ludlow. Meet me down in the main mine near the face tomorrow at 3:00. We'll take care of the spies then. I'm sure

they'll be unlucky and have a terrible accident tomorrow. You know what to do.

Parker

Julia's breath caught in her throat. She kept walking and folded the note back the way it was before it sprang open in front of her eyes.

"Mr. Parker is going to cause an accident in the mine tomorrow," whispered Julia. "He's going to hurt some people because they're in the union, and Mr. Evans is going to do it with him!"

Teddy must not have known this note was hidden in the mail, thought Julia. I only found it because it fell out when he threw the letters at me, and I had to pick them up off the ground. I shouldn't know about Mr. Parker's plans. I shouldn't know, but I do!

# The Hiding Place

"**M**aybe Teddy wrote this note to play a trick on me, an awful trick!" Julia said to herself. She looked at the note again.

"No," said Julia. "Teddy doesn't write this neatly. Besides, we write in pencil at school and this is written in ink."

Who else knows about his note besides me? wondered Julia. The person who wrote this terrible message knows, I know, and Mrs. Evans will know when I give it to her, if I give it to her. If I don't give this to Mrs. Evans, she can't give it to her husband. Then Mr. Evans won't know what he is supposed to do tomorrow. He'll never know!

I know, but I have to act like I don't. I have to act normal, thought Julia.

"I'm walking and everything is regular," said Julia to herself.

Julia's toe hit a rock as she came to a fork in the road. She kept her balance and continued walking. She saw the small Phippsburg store in the distance to her left and headed toward it. Her feet felt numb from crunching snow under thin shoes. It was like shuffling on two blocks of ice. Julia looked at the thick trees around her for signs of blue.

No, it's too cold for Teddy Parker to be spying on me now, she thought.

He paid me to deliver his letters and I will. I'm sure Teddy doesn't know about the note or he wouldn't have given it to me in the stack of letters. Maybe Mr. Parker sends notes to Mr. Evans about the mine all of the time. Maybe Teddy delivers notes and doesn't know that he's a messenger. Maybe Teddy is testing me to see if I'll deliver this note. Maybe Mr. Parker thinks Papa is a spy for the union and he's planning to hurt Papa. I can't let it happen! I can't let Mr. Parker cause an accident!

Julia looked around frantically for a place to bury the note. She dug at the snow. It was frozen solid. Her fingers couldn't break through the crust.

Even if I could dig a hole, someone will find this note when the snow melts in a few months. It might get back to Mr. Parker, and he'll ask Teddy how his note ended up out here. Teddy could say he dropped it, but he'll probably tell his father that he asked me to deliver it. Mr. Parker will make Papa pay one way or another.

Julia's fingers were already folding the note before she realized that she was doing it. She folded it into a small square. She looked at it and instantly knew the only thing that she could do. Julia bent down and unlaced her shoe. She slipped Mr. Parker's note under her foot in the right shoe. It was the one without a hole in the bottom. She pushed the note under the ball of her foot near the toe so it wouldn't work its way out.

Julia didn't know what she would do with the note later, but she did know that she was not going to deliver it to

Mrs. Evans. She would make sure Mr. Evans did not get Mr. Parker's message. She laced up her shoe and tied a bow.

I'm helping the union now. I'm working against Mr. Parker to protect the union spies and the miners. I wonder if this makes me a union spy, thought Julia. She smiled for a moment. My wish for something exciting is coming true. It is magic!

"This is not boring at all! Being a spy is definitely something out of the ordinary!" said Julia to herself.

The fear of having something happen to Papa swelled up inside her and dissolved her smile. An injured or a dead miner would mean nothing to Mr. Parker. Phippsburg was no different from Ludlow. The mine owners had all of the power.

Julia straightened up and started walking again. I have a tiny bit of power right here in this note. Teddy Parker threw a teensy bit of power right at me! A little bit of Mr. Parker's power is in my control right now. A gram of a mine owner's power is inside of my shoe and I'm walking on it! The note made a lump under Julia's right toes, but her feet were so numb she could hardly feel it.

In a few minutes she would be inside the warm store. Maybe she could take her time getting the things for Mama. It wouldn't be fun seeing Mrs. Evans, but it would give her feet a chance to warm up a bit.

Julia spotted the outline of a woman in the store window. The woman was watching her.

# The Store

J ulia pretended not to notice that Mrs. Evans was
watching her make her way across the snow and
into the store. Julia calmed her fears by telling
herself that she was too far away when she tucked
the note into her shoe for Mrs. Evans to see her.

"Mrs. Evans would have to be an eagle to see that far," said
Julia to herself.

Julia set the expression on her face. She had to act
normal. She looked straight ahead at the door to the store,
pushed it open, and walked in.

Julia loved the way it smelled inside. Aromas of sugar,
flour, cereal grains, butter, dried meats, honey, and molasses
mixed to fill the air.

"Julia," said Mrs. Evans turning from the window to
face her.

"Hi, Mrs. Evans," Julia said.

Julia gazed at the picture of Mr. and Mrs. Evans standing
with Mr. Parker on the wall behind the cash register. They
smiled in front of the sign that said "Phippsburg Store."

Mrs. Evans probably passed the notes from Mr. Parker to Mr. Evans after she read them, of course.

"Teddy Parker asked me to put these letters in the mail for him," said Julia.

Mrs. Evans frowned. She squinted at Julia as if she was trying to find a microscopic object in Julia's eyes.

"Humph!" said Mrs. Evans. "Give them to me."

Julia handed her the pile. She watched Mrs. Evans rifle through the envelopes.

She's looking for it, thought Julia. She's looking for the note. She's done this many times before. Mr. Parker must pass messages to Mr. Evans this way every day. I have to look polite and bored.

Julia began reciting the multiplication tables of 8 in her head so she wouldn't think about the note.

"3x8 is 24. 4x8 is 32. 5x8 is 40. 6x8 is 48. 7x8 is… ."

"Is this all that Teddy gave you?" asked Mrs. Evans, interrupting Julia's thoughts.

"Yes, Ma'am," said Julia as innocently as she could. She hoped that Mrs. Evans couldn't hear her heart pounding through Mama's coat. The beating was deafening in Julia's ears.

"I'll put these letters in the box for the postman when he comes tomorrow," said Mrs. Evans.

Julia nodded. She watched Mrs. Evans put the envelopes one by one through the slot on top of a wooden box marked "U.S. Mail."

"What do you need today?" asked Mrs. Evans.

Julia studied Mrs. Evans's tight lips and realized that they might not be elastic enough to stretch into a smile.

"Mama wants some milk, two cans of tomatoes, and a piece of ham, please," said Julia.

"You'll have to wait a few minutes while I fill a bottle of milk for you from the cans in the back ice box. I'll cut you a piece of ham from back there, too. Don't touch anything in the store. I'll know it if you do," said Mrs. Evans, pointing her bony index finger at Julia.

# The Headlines

**"I** won't touch anything," said Julia.

Mama told Julia that she thought the prices in the Phippsburg store were too high, but there was no other store in town. The store, like everything else, was owned by the mine. It seemed like the store took back every cent the mine paid its workers.

Julia heard Mrs. Evans moving heavy milk cans and blocks of ice behind the wall. Her eyes scanned the counter, but her hands touched nothing. She saw a small stack of newspapers to her right. She couldn't help but notice *The Rocky Mountain News* headlines for Tuesday, April 21, 1914. Julia read:

"THIRTEEN KILLED IN BATTLE AT LUDLOW; STRIKERS' TENT COLONY BURNED."

Julia controlled a gasp. Who could be killing miners in Ludlow? She read on.

A smaller caption read:

"1,500 ARMED MINERS RUSHING IN TO EXTERMINATE GUARDSMEN.

Fighting Rages 14 Hours and Small Force of
Militia Sweeps Hills With Machine Guns to Hold
Back Determined Band of Union Workers."

This sounds like the miners have turned into an army,
thought Julia. Fifteen hundred miners is ten times the amount
we have in Phippsburg. I wonder what they were armed
with? Surely some shovels and picks are no match for
machine guns!

Julia strained her eyes to make out more of the report:

> "Thirteen dead, scores injured, the Ludlow
> strikers' tent colony burned and hundreds of
> women and children homeless was the result
> up to midnight of one of the bloodiest battles in
> labor welfare ever waged in the West. Four
> hundred striking miners were entrenched in the
> hills back of Ludlow this morning awaiting daylight
> to wipe out 177 members of the state National
> Guard, with whom they fought for fourteen hours
> yesterday."

The newspaper makes it sound like the miners are
attacking the National Guard, thought Julia. The Guard
was supposed to be protecting the miners. Papa said that
the National Guard switched sides and is working for the
mine owners. Why do they have to shoot miners? Why
can't the mine owners talk things out with the workers?

Papa is right. We don't want this kind of trouble here.
Now Mr. Parker is already planning to make it look like some
miners in Phippsburg got hurt in an accident. Mr. Parker
must think that Ludlow gives him permission to start
killing people, too!

43

Julia read a smaller article headline:

"President Wilson Asked to Intervene by Miners
and All in Colonies Are Urged to Arm to
Protect Themselves—Many Gather in Hills."

What's happened in Ludlow is much more serious than
Frank O'Malley told me today, Julia thought. The miners are
supposed to get weapons to protect themselves. How can they
do that living outside in tents? I'll bet Frank doesn't know
about this.

"I wonder if Papa knows that the president of the United
States is getting involved in this strike?" Julia asked herself.

"What are you looking at?" said Mrs. Evans, coming back
to the counter.

"Nothing, Ma'am," said Julia.

"You can't read all of those English words in the newspapers, can you?" asked Mrs. Evans.

"Oh, no, Ma'am," said Julia. "I'm working real hard at
school, but Teacher hasn't taught us how to read anything
like that."

Julia wasn't lying. Teacher hadn't taught her to read the
newspaper. Julia figured out how to read it on her own. She
often skimmed the headlines when she visited the store.

Julia heard Papa's voice in her head telling her that it was
dangerous to speak out against the mine. Mrs. Evans was the
mine to Julia right now, and Julia was tiptoeing carefully on
thin ice. Julia felt like she was in a cage with a dangerous
animal. She wondered if Papa knew that people were getting
killed in Ludlow. It was already Thursday and the newspaper
was two days old. Maybe Papa knew. Anyway, he would not
want to hear this kind of news from his daughter.

44

Julia felt the danger of Ludlow in her stomach. She decided not to tell anyone about what she had seen in the paper. She put it far back in her mind and tried to forget it was there.

"Well, you Italians don't need to worry about newspapers. They're for us Americans," said Mrs. Evans.

Something inside of Julia started to boil like a tea kettle. Julia had to snuff the flame before the whistle started screaming.

"Yes, Ma'am," said Julia calmly, as if she were talking to a coiled rattlesnake.

She glanced at the newspaper again to be sure it didn't say that you had to be American to read it. It didn't have any words like that on the front page.

Mrs. Evans put the frosty milk with two cans of tomatoes stacked on top of each other in an empty flour sack. She wrapped the ham in brown paper and stuck it on top of the tomatoes. Mrs. Evans held out her hand. Julia put the coins Mama had given to her in Mrs. Evans' ice cold palm. Julia noted that Mrs. Evans' eyes were colder than the hand, which took Mama's coins. Mrs. Evans put Mama's money into a black cash register and dug for change. Then she pushed Mama's change into Julia's hand.

Julia dropped the change into Mama's coat pocket along with Teddy's dime. She grabbed the flour sack full of groceries.

"Thank you, Mrs. Evans. Have a nice evening," said Julia. Mrs. Evans nodded.

Julia had made it into and out of the store with Mr. Parker's note hidden safely inside her shoe. She tightened her coat, walked outside, and headed home. She thought of the yellow house. Julia looked down at the frozen road.

It was the same road. It was the same walk. It was the
same errand to get groceries for Mama, thought Julia, but
everything was not the same.

# The Spy

J ulia felt the lump in her right shoe where the folded note was hidden. Maybe my wish for today to be different is making things happen, thought Julia. Teddy Parker lied and made me take his punishment at school. Then he paid me a whole dime to do his chores and bring his family's mail to the store. Now I have a note from Mr. Parker hidden in my shoe. I know that Mr. Parker is planning an accident at the mine tomorrow. I've stopped his message from getting to Mr. Evans, and I'm helping the union like the spies working in the mine. Now I'm a spy, too!

I have to try and stop Mr. Parker from hurting the union workers. They are trying to help all of the miners, including Papa. It would be a good thing if they could get Mr. Parker to make improvements at the mine. The union workers would never believe that a girl helped them, maybe even saved their lives, but it's true! It's up to me, Julia the spy!

"What do union spies do?" Julia asked herself as she walked home. They keep secrets for one thing, thought Julia as she felt the note under her toes every other step she took.

Julia thought about how Teddy Parker regularly acted up at school. He never changes. He's Mr. Parker's son. Mr. Parker isn't going to change either.

"He isn't going to listen to the union workers," said Julia. "He's going to create an accident with or without Mr. Evans. I haven't stopped him yet. I could show Papa this note. Maybe he can stop Mr. Parker."

Julia slid open the door to their boxcar.

"Hi, Mama. Here are your groceries and your change," said Julia.

She hung Mama's coat on a hook near the door.

"Take off your shoes and warm your feet," said Mama.

Panic hit Julia in the chest and her heart skipped a beat.

"My feet aren't too cold now," Julia lied.

It was the second time in her life that Julia had lied. Her mouth went dry, and her throat felt like she was swallowing cotton.

Mama can't see the note I took and hid in my shoe. Now I can't tell Papa about Mr. Parker's note, thought Julia. Then Mama will know I lied, but worse than that, it might be too dangerous for Papa! Julia imagined Papa at the mine tomorrow showing Mr. Parker the note. Teddy and I will both be punished. Mr. Parker will still go through with his plan for an accident. Papa will be fired. This is very dangerous.

Papa will never forgive me if he finds out I lied, but I have to keep the note a secret.

Spies keep secrets and tell lies, thought Julia. At least it isn't a regular boring night. If only I wasn't scared half to death!

Julia played with Angela and Lucia. She had sewn dolls for them out of scraps of material. They played like they were taking care of their babies. It calmed Julia's nerves and made her stomach stop doing flips to play with her sisters.

A few minutes before 6:00 Julia told her sisters, "Take care of our babies. I have to help Mama now."

She picked up a bucket and put on Mama's coat. She slid open the boxcar door wide enough for her and the bucket to pass through, wide enough to keep the stove heat in and the frigid night air out.

Julia looked for soft snow. Everything was frozen. She used the bucket to break the frozen crust. She hit it again and again until the bucket dug in and filled three quarters of the way with snow. At least the snow brings water to our front door. It's easier than walking all the way to the well.

Julia stood up and exhaled all of her air into a puffy cloud.

"I'm a train," she said, puffing three more times. She giggled for a moment. Julia took a step and felt the lump in her shoe.

"What am I going to do about tomorrow?" Julia asked herself.

It was too cold to stay outside another second. Julia lugged the heavy bucket back into the boxcar. She carefully opened the door again only wide enough to fit herself and the snow-filled bucket through the opening. Julia hung up Mama's coat.

"Let me touch the snow," begged Angela.

"Hurry," said Julia.

Angela and Lucia each grabbed small handfuls of snow.

"It's freezing!" squealed Angela.

Lucia dropped her snow quickly and rubbed her miniature hands on her front.

"Put it back now, Angela. I have to make Papa's water," said Julia.

Angela put the snow back and touched her own cheeks. Julia figured it must be fun to feel the cold when you'd been inside near the stove all day.

Julia scooped the snow into a pan on the stove. She watched it turn to liquid at the edges. Soon it would be warm enough for washing Papa's face and hands. If Papa was late Julia would pull the water off the stove so it wouldn't get too hot and burn him, but he still had a while to get home before all of the snow melted.

Mama poured noodles into boiling water in a pot next to Papa's washing water. Papa would be home in fifteen minutes, ten if he walked fast.

Julia shifted her weight off the foot with the note in the shoe. I wish I knew what to do with this note. I wish I could stop Mr. Parker's accident just by wishing. I have all night to come up with a plan. Someone has to stop Mr. Parker, someone who accidentally found a note meant for somebody else, someone who knows Mr. Parker's plans, someone like me: Julia Iannacito!

# The Plan

"Papa's home!" yelled Angela.

"Bella!" exclaimed Papa, lifting Angela in the air. "My beautiful girls!" He held Angela on one side and reached out his other arm. Julia, Lucia, and Mama took turns hugging Papa.

Papa's clothes felt like winter, and he smelled like the coal mine. Papa's red sweater felt rough and scratchy against Julia's face.

"Let me wash my hands and face," said Papa.

"Your water should be just right, Papa," said Julia.

She took the pan off the flame and set it on a folded cloth. She watched Papa plunge his hands into the water and splash his face again and again. He rubbed a broken bar of soap between his large hands. Julia watched gray soap bubbles fall into the pan. Papa scrubbed his face and then rinsed off. He dried his face on a towel. When he looked up his face was flesh-colored again, and the water was gray-black.

Julia slid open the door and threw the water out into the night. She imagined it froze before it hit the ground.

She wondered if she would be able to hear the ice break as it hit the frozen snow, but she slid the door shut too soon to find out.

"Let's eat," said Papa.

Mama put the macaroni and sauce on the table. Julia put half a loaf of bread next to it. Julia, her sisters, Papa, and Mama made a close circle around the table in the middle of the boxcar.

"We give thanks for our blessings, Amen," said Papa.

The first mouthful of Mama's noodles and sauce woke up Julia's taste buds.

She watched Angela suck in a single noodle. It looked like a worm disappearing into its hole in the soil.

"Julia, cut Lucia's macaroni," said Mama.

Julia used Lucia's spoon to cut her long noodles into manageable, three-year-old bites.

"How was the mine today?" Mama asked.

"It was the same as always. This morning I loaded coal at the take out," said Papa. "Then, Mr. Parker had a few of us go down and work near the face where they cut the coal. It was cold and dark down near the face."

Julia almost choked on her second bite of pasta. "Where will you work tomorrow?" she asked.

"What's this sudden interest in where I'm working," asked Papa.

"I just want to know," said Julia.

"Unless I hear different, I'll be cutting coal near the face again," said Papa.

Julia's insides whirled. Papa can't be anywhere near the face tomorrow in case Mr. Parker goes through with his plan for an accident. Julia's mind raced around one idea and then another.

"Papa, where does Mr. Evans work at the mine?" she asked.

"Mr. Evans doesn't work at the mine. He runs errands for Mr. Parker like bringing supplies from the store. He delivers messages to crews working at different spots," said Papa. "Why do you care about Mr. Evans?"

"I..." Julia had to think fast. "I was at the store for Mama today and I saw his picture so I wondered what Mr. Evans does."

Papa nodded as he dug into his second bowl of macaroni. Julia ate without tasting her food. She wriggled her toes over the note in her shoe.

"There's one errand Mr. Evans won't be doing for Mr. Parker tomorrow," said Julia to herself. "But Mr. Parker can still hurt a lot of people without Mr. Evans's help. I haven't stopped the accident yet. There must be some way to get Papa back to his old job of loading coal on the outside."

Everyone was finishing dinner and sopping up the last drops of sauce with torn pieces of bread.

"Julia, take your sisters to the outhouse. It's almost time for bed," said Mama.

Julia shoveled the last bite of dinner into her mouth. She grabbed Mama's coat and put it on in one fluid motion. Angela held a blanket wrapped around herself. Julia took a quilt off the girls' bed and wrapped it around Lucia.

"Here's the bucket. You can bring snow for the dishes on your way back," said Mama.

Julia held the bucket handle with one hand and Lucia with the other. Angela slid open the boxcar door and they

53

scurried toward the outhouse. When they got there, someone was already inside.

"Jump up and down to keep warm, Angela," said Julia. She ran in place and rubbed Lucia's back and arms through the blanket.

In a few minutes, Mr. Zarlingo opened the door and stepped out.

"Buona sera," he said.

"Buona sera, good evening, Mr. Zarlingo" said Julia.

The girls ducked inside and took turns sitting on the bone cold hole in the wooden bench.

"Let's go," said Julia, as soon as they had all finished.

They scurried back to the boxcar. Julia got her sisters inside and then chipped at the crusted snow with the side of her bucket. Soon she had scooped up a bucketful. The night air was so cold that the hairs inside Julia's nose froze. It felt like breathing through tiny wooden slivers.

Julia pulled her hand into Mama's coat sleeve like a turtle drawing its head into its shell. Julia used the sleeve like a glove to hold onto the freezing bucket handle. She darted back to the warmth of the boxcar. She scooped snow into a pot on the stove before hanging up Mama's coat. Soon she would enjoy washing her family's dishes in the coal-heated water.

"Help me get the girls into bed," said Mama.

Julia helped Angela put on her night clothes. She worked her toes over the note in her shoe.

"The night's passing too quickly," said Julia to herself. "I have to come up with a plan soon."

Papa slid open the door and went to visit the outhouse.

"Leave me some room on the end of the bed, you two," said Julia.

"We want you in the middle," said Angela.

"Sleep together now to stay warm. I'll snuggle into the middle when I come to bed," said Julia.

"Do you promise?" asked Angela.

"I promise," said Julia. She kissed them each on the forehead.

Julia saw steam rising from the water pot. Papa walked back into the boxcar. He pulled off his red sweater and hung it next to Mama's coat. Papa slid the blanket, sewed onto a rope strung across the boxcar, to close off his and Mama's bed. Julia heard him taking off his boots and changing into his nightshirt. She heard blankets moving and knew Papa was getting into bed.

Julia divided the heated water into two pots and put a little soap in one of them. She washed dishes in the soapy pot and rinsed them in the plain water pot. Mama came back into the boxcar rubbing her arms.

"It's freezing and I had to wait for Mrs. Brunetti to finish out there," said Mama.

Julia dried the dishes and stacked them in a wooden crate on the back wall.

"We had to wait a minute out there, too," said Julia.

"There's a little mending in the laundry bag for Mrs. Parker. Do it quickly and go to bed," said Mama.

"How many pieces?" asked Julia.

"There's three of Mr. Parker's socks and a pair of Teddy's pants. I left them on top for you," said Mama. "Good night Julia. I'm going to bed to warm up."

Julia opened the bag and pulled out the socks and pants. Soon she heard Papa snoring.

Julia bent close to the oil lamp to thread her needle. She started sewing. The needle went in and out of a sock like her mind went in and out of possibilities. She stitched her loose thoughts together like the material in her hand. Julia knotted the last stitch in Mr. Parker's sock at the same moment she secured her plan. She cut the thread with her teeth.

Julia reached down and took the note out of her shoe.

"It's time for me to write a note of my own," Julia whispered.

# The Note

J ulia took a pen out of the crate next to their dishes. She picked up Mr. Parker's note. He had left several inches of unused paper on the bottom. A person had to be rich to waste paper like that, thought Julia. She carefully folded a crease to separate the used paper from the unused paper. She tore along the fold. She studied Mr. Parker's note.

Julia decided if she signed her note from Mr. Parker someone could take it to him. He would know he did not write it, and then he would want to know who did. Papa might not ever get the message to leave the face, but if she wrote it from Mr. Evans it would be less important. It wouldn't be questioned. It would have a better chance of being delivered.

Julia printed carefully:

Tell Mike Cito to leave the face and load coal
after lunch today. – Mr. Evans

Now Julia had a note of her own. She folded it and put it in her shoe where Mr. Parker's note had been. Next she had to find a way to get it to the mine so someone could fetch

Papa away from the face. Girls weren't allowed at the mine. It was considered bad luck.

"I need to get a boy to deliver this note, said Julia to herself. There is one boy who will help me. There's a boy who might be willing to be a union spy, too. I'll ask Frank O'Malley to do it. He understands all about the union, and the mine, and Mr. Parker. Frank and I can do it together. I could go with him at lunch recess," said Julia to herself. "We'll slip away while everyone else is playing games outside. We'll run to the mine. I'll hide in the woods near the mine and watch to make sure Frank delivers the note. We'll run back before recess break is over. If we're late, we'll be punished. It will be a terrible punishment for a boy and a girl to be late together. We'll run our fastest. We can't be late! First, we'll have to make sure that Mr. Evans is nowhere in sight. Frank will hand my note to a miner who can read English. The miner will go into the mine and find Papa. He'll tell him Mr. Evans wants him to leave the face and load coal. Even if Mr. Parker goes through with his accident, Papa won't be near the face when it happens."

Julia had it all sorted out in her head. Her plan had to work. It was the only possible way she could think of to get Papa out of the mine.

"A note for a note, and a plan for a plan, Mr. Parker," said Julia. She packed the Parkers' laundry for tomorrow. She placed her shoes at the edge of the box bed. She checked to make sure her note was still in her right shoe. She felt it folded safely in its hiding spot near the toe.

There was one thing left to do. Julia picked up Mr. Parker's note from the table. She looked at it for the last time before she opened the door on the coal stove. Julia threw Mr. Parker's note onto the red, hot coals. It caught fire immediately. She watched the paper burn and curl.

Mr. Parker's message to Mr. Evans was gone forever. The note that Teddy had carelessly tossed at Julia, the note that ended up hidden in Julia's right shoe, the note that made Julia have to save Papa from danger turned to ash in the boxcar's coal stove. Only Mr. Parker and Julia knew what it said. Only Julia knew what had to be done tomorrow.

Julia changed her clothes and crawled into bed between her sleeping sisters. She welcomed their slumbering warmth.

Julia drifted to sleep. In her dreams, she and Frank O'Malley ran through the woods to the mine.

# The Delivery

Julia and Frank raced across the schoolyard. The door was closed. They opened it and threw themselves inside.

"Julia! Frank! Where have you been?" demanded Miss Crawford. "You're late!"

Julia opened her mouth to speak, but no sound came out.

She smelled coffee and woke with a start. Papa and Mama sat at the table. Julia watched Papa take a bite of bread and ham. He and Mama sipped black coffee. Julia got up carefully so she wouldn't wake her sisters. She pulled on her clothes and stepped into her shoes. Her note bunched up at the toe and Julia had to take her shoe off and adjust it so it lay smoothly.

She ate bread with Papa.

"It's time for me to go," he said. He leaned down and gave Julia a kiss on each eyelid with coffee-warmed lips. Papa kissed Mama goodbye. He picked up his packed lunch, slipped his red sweater on over his two shirts and stepped out of the boxcar.

Julia braided her hair. She pulled on Mama's coat.

"I will see you after school, Mama," said Julia, kissing her cheek.

"Don't forget to take the Parkers' laundry. You can drop it off on your way home from school," said Mama.

Julia flung the Parkers' bag over her shoulder and stepped out of the boxcar. The sun was peeking out over the mountains and lit up Phippsburg.

It started out ordinary like yesterday and like every other day before it, but Julia knew this day would be the most unordinary day in her life. She had a big job to do. She was going to break the school rules for the first time in her life and she was going to get Frank to help her.

Julia thought about the children of the mining families in Ludlow. Did they start out their day on April 20 just like every other day? Did they have any idea what terrible things were about to happen?

Julia decided that they didn't know. She decided that no child from Ludlow found a note telling of someone's plan to start shooting at people. She decided that no child had a chance to make a plan of their own to stop a mine owner from doing a horrible thing. But Julia had a chance to change things in Phippsburg. Julia had to break the school rules today and take a chance to change things at the mine, at least for her Papa!

The morning sun shone brightly now. It lit the frozen snow crystals, making them sparkle like diamonds.

Julia didn't feel the weight of the Parkers' laundry bag today. Much more serious matters were heavy on her mind. Julia walked as quickly as she could without slipping on icy spots. She made her way along the Yampa River. Soon she heard the other students playing and laughing in the school-yard. Julia trotted the rest of the way to school. She looked for Frank.

Julia didn't see him. The boys had a game of freeze tag going. Frank was not in the group.

"Frank, where are you?" said Julia to herself.

Girls were joining the tag game.

"We have to run to stay warm," said a second grader as she zipped past.

Julia didn't dare put the Parkers' laundry bag on the ground. It might get wet and dirty. She hopped up and down to stay warm.

"I wonder what time it is," said Julia to herself. "It must be almost 8:30. Where can Frank be? I can't get my message to Papa without him."

Miss Crawford stepped out of the schoolhouse and rang the bell. The students lined up from smallest to biggest. Julia turned to look for Frank at the back of the line. He wasn't there. The line moved slowly into the schoolhouse. Julia looked back again. A second before the door closed she saw Frank slip inside. Everyone took off their coats and hats and hung them on nails poking out of the back wall.

Julia hung Mama's coat over the Parkers' laundry bag.

"Frank," she whispered.

"No talking," said Miss Crawford.

Julia looked at Frank. He looked back at her and shrugged. Julia couldn't say anything more without getting into trouble.

"Take your seats," said Miss Crawford.

Julia had to think of how to let Frank know that she needed him to go with her during recess. Everyone was writing their spelling words on their tablets.

"I could write Frank a note," said Julia to herself. "If I get caught I'll have to spend recess with my nose on the board. Then I won't be able to go with Frank. I could get the note in my shoe to him and he could run it to the mine by himself. No, I need to go to see that Frank delivers the note to somebody who can get the message to Papa. What if Frank won't do it? I have to try. It's a huge risk, but what choice do I have?"

Julia lifted the pages of her tablet keeping the back page hidden. On the bottom of it she wrote:

> Frank,
>
> Meet me at recess. We have to take care of something.
>
> Julia

She carefully tore the bottom strip off the last page and folded it in the palm of her hand. The other fifth grader who didn't speak English watched her. Julia kept her note to Frank hidden in her hand.

Julia was sweating even though it was cold in the schoolroom.

"You have five minutes to finish your spelling," said Miss Crawford. "We will work on reading next."

Julia glanced around her to see who she could pass her note to in order to get it to Frank. Her eyes met Teddy's. He smirked at her. Julia faced front again.

"It's too dangerous to pass this note," she said to herself. "It would be a disaster if Teddy got a hold of it. Besides, no one has ever passed notes before in Miss Crawford's class. I would surely get caught! I'll have to deliver it myself."

# The Chosen One

J ulia raised her hand.

"What is it, Julia?" asked Miss Crawford.

"May I be excused to use the outhouse?" asked Julia.

"The morning just started. Is this an emergency?" demanded Miss Crawford.

"Yes, Ma'am, it is," said Julia. She felt relieved that she didn't have to completely lie now. It was a real emergency!

"Go quickly," said Miss Crawford.

Julia stood up, turned and walked toward the back. How could she pass her note to Frank with everyone including Miss Crawford watching her? At least her back was turned to the teacher.

Julia stared at Frank. He searched her eyes for a clue as to what was happening. Julia walked straight toward him and purposely twisted her ankle so she fell against Frank.

"Whoa!" said Frank, breaking Julia's fall.

Julia pressed her note into his hand.

Frank closed his fingers around it instinctively.

"Ha, ha. What a clumsy thing you are," said Teddy.

"Excuse me," said Julia acting embarrassed. She ran out of the building. Inside the outhouse, Julia caught her breath.

"Please let my plan work," she prayed.

Julia counted to thirty, stepped out of the outhouse and walked back into the school.

Everyone looked at her for a moment and then turned back to their reading books. Julia looked at Frank. He nodded once.

"Frank got my message. He understands. We'll meet at recess. I'll tell him my plan and we'll get to the mine as quickly as we can," said Julia to herself.

She sat down and opened her book. Julia kept her eyes on the page, but she wasn't reading. She couldn't concentrate. She went through the schedule of events that would happen during recess over and over in her mind.

"Julia," said Miss Crawford.

"What?" asked Julia.

There were snickers from the back. Julia guessed that it was Teddy.

"It's your turn to read. Please begin," said Miss Crawford.

Julia had no idea what she was supposed to read. She had to try to cover the fact that she wasn't paying attention.

"Where would you like me to start?" asked Julia.

"Start where you left off yesterday, of course," replied Miss Crawford.

Julia smiled. She remembered the last words she read yesterday in her *McGuffey's Reader* by William Holmes McGuffey, and quickly found her place.

"'As soon as Jack found there were oranges in the baskets, he determined to have one, and going up to the basket, he slipped in his hand and took out one of the largest, and was making off with it.'" read Julia.

"That was fine, Julia," said Miss Crawford.

Teddy struggled with, "'Not I, said Jack, as I am the largest, I shall do as I please.' Miss Crawford, is that enough?" he asked.

"It's fine, Teddy," said Miss Crawford. "Frank, please finish Teddy's part for him."

"'But Charles was not afraid, and taking the orange out of his hand, he threw it back into the basket,'" read Frank.

Their voices were drowned out by the ocean of thoughts in Julia's own head. She calculated the minutes until she and Frank would be running to the mine. Exactly thirty-six minutes, forty-seven seconds until lunch and recess.

Why does time crawl when we are waiting for something to happen? wondered Julia. I'm sure time will seem to speed by when Frank and I are traveling to the mine and back in just thirty minutes.

Julia skimmed the lines in her book. She thought it was interesting that Teddy read the part about taking the oranges and Frank read the part about putting them back. It seemed like they were each assigned the right part.

At last, the morning lessons were finished.

"It's time to get ready for lunch, boys and girls," said Miss Crawford. "Get out your food and eat. You have fifteen minutes to eat before we begin our recess break out in the schoolyard."

Julia sat at her seat and unwrapped the bread Mama had packed for her. There was a piece of ham left over from Papa's breakfast. Julia ate. She chewed and swallowed even though she had no appetite. She knew she would need the strength from the food to run in a few minutes. She finished and waited politely until Miss Crawford dismissed everyone.

"It's about time to take a break. Before you go outside, I need some helpers during recess."

Miss Crawford always picked Teddy Parker to stay in and help her. Julia wished Miss Crawford would pick her even one time. It would be nice to be treated special by the teacher, but today Julia was glad to have Teddy Parker get special treatment. That way he wouldn't notice when she and Frank slipped away into the woods in the direction of his father's mine.

"I need two students to stay in and help me clean the chalkboard. I also need help bringing coal in from the shed out back, since our stove is running low. Then we have some supplies that Mr. Evans from the store delivered to us before school this morning. I ordered some books and paper that finally came in by mail yesterday. Who wants to help?" said Miss Crawford.

Hands went up throughout the third, fourth, and sixth graders. The girl who didn't speak English never raised her hand. Julia couldn't raise her own hand today. She was busy during recess. Miss Crawford would never choose her anyway. Everyone knew it would be Teddy Parker who would be chosen.

"Let's see, we have so many wonderful volunteers," said Miss Crawford.

It's the same thing she always says, thought Julia, right before she chooses Teddy Parker. She will most likely pick Paulina Parker for her second helper. Maybe Miss Crawford will even get a bonus from Mr. Parker for picking his children.

"How good of you to volunteer, Teddy," said Miss Crawford. "Of course you will stay in and help me. How about you, Paulina? Would you like to stay and help too?"

"No, thank you," said Paulina. "Nellie and I are counting on playing at recess."

"Of course you are," said Miss Crawford.

Teddy and Paulina are the only ones who would dare say no to the teacher, thought Julia. I guess when you get treated special all of the time you get filled up with specialness. Then you don't need any more. I've just never been filled up with it yet. I've never been filled up even a little, but today I'm filling myself up. I have a special thing to do so there's no room inside of me for Miss Crawford's specialness. She can go ahead and pick some other person.

Miss Crawford eyed the students. "We will need one more person to help us."

The teacher's eyes stopped moving. Julia watched her narrow her focus.

"Let's see, yes, Frank, Frank O'Malley will do. I will count on Frank and Teddy to stay in and help me during recess."

# The Disguise

"**F**rank O'Malley!" Julia almost said out loud. This was all wrong! What was Miss Crawford thinking? Julia turned and looked hard at Frank. He shrugged. Now what could Julia do? Her whole plan counted on Frank to take her note to the mine. She needed a boy. What other boy could help her?

I wish I was a silly ole boy myself, thought Julia. She had to think. Her classmates were finishing their meager lunches. It was almost time for recess. Something had to be done.

Julia looked over the other boys in the class. There was no one else who could do the job, no one else she trusted, no one else to help her Papa, no one else but Julia herself!

That settled it. Julia was going to the mine by herself. She didn't quite know what would happen at the mine since no girls were allowed, but she was going.

"Class is dismissed," said Miss Crawford. "Get your coats and go outside."

Julia lifted Mama's coat off the hook where it covered the Parkers' laundry bag. She remembered sewing socks and Teddy's pants last night while her family and most likely the

Parker family slept. Teddy was lucky to have more than one pair of pants so he could be wearing a pair while another pair sat in the laundry bag.

"Teddy's pants are in this bag," said Julia to herself. "That's it! He doesn't need them right now, but I do!"

She clutched the Parkers' laundry bag in her hand and headed for the door. She glanced at Frank's coat and hat hanging on their hook.

"Frank's clothes can help me even if he can't! I hope Frank won't mind if I borrow these," she said. "I'll have them back here before he needs them, since he's not going out for recess."

Julia stuffed Frank's coat inside of Mama's big coat next to her chest. She held it in place with her arm. She jammed Frank's hat in Mama's coat pocket. Julia caught Paulina's eye. Paulina stuck her tongue out at Julia. They must practice being mean in that family, thought Julia, or maybe it just comes natural with their privileged position.

No one else seemed to notice Julia at all. They were busy getting bundled up and heading out the door. Recess was always a necessary relief after sitting like statues through the school day.

Julia ran out the door and made her way to edge of the schoolyard. She looked around. The other girl in her grade watched her for a minute and then turned to play with some younger children. Paulina Parker was busy with Nellie. Julia darted into the trees and found a hiding place.

She took off Mama's coat. It was freezing, but Julia was sweating. She yanked Teddy's pants out of the laundry bag and stepped into them. They were big, but Julia stuffed her skirt into the waist. She buttoned the pants round her own clothes. Next she put on Frank's coat. She tucked her hair up into his hat and pulled it down over her ears. She put Mama's coat on the ground and set the Parkers' laundry bag on top of it. It was the best she could do to keep it clean.

Julia hoped she looked enough like a boy to deliver the note. It was securely folded inside her shoe. She began to run. She ran through the trees, weaving in and out of snow-covered aspen. She should be at the mine in about twelve minutes if she didn't stop.

Julia ran and ran. She gasped for air. Her nerves made her get winded long before she normally would. She concentrated on her breath and tried to suck it in more evenly. She skidded over an icy spot. Her toes were numb. She couldn't feel the note inside her shoe any longer, but it had to be there.

After what seemed like an hour of running, Julia heard the sound of shovels scooping coal and knew that she was close to the mine. She had been here before in the summer when she hid in the trees and watched the miners work. She never let herself be seen so she wouldn't cause bad luck. She wouldn't be seen today either. She was a schoolboy with a note from Mr. Evans. She was delivering a message and leaving.

Julia slowed down to catch her breath. She bent down, unlaced, and took off her right shoe. She reached inside. There was nothing there!

Julia plunged her hand into her shoe again. She frantically fished around the toe for her note. Something came loose. She pulled it out. It was her folded note. It had gotten pressed into the toe of her shoe. She put her shoe on and laced it up.

"That was close," she said.

She breathed in and out deeply for five breaths. Julia made sure her hair was tucked up inside of Frank's hat. She was thankful for braids instead of rag curls today. Braids were easier to hide. She pulled the hat down over her head and face. Julia stood with her legs apart like a boy and squarely jogged out into the open.

A few miners looked up and then went back to loading coal. This is where she had hoped Papa would be working instead of inside the mine near the face. Julia held the note up. She would not be able to speak. Someone might recognize the voice of a girl. Julia spit on the ground like the older boys at school.

She waved the note now. A miner looked at her and shook his head. Julia thought he might not like her spitting. Then the miner said something in Greek to another man. Julia nodded. She definitely needed someone who spoke English to read her note. The Greek miner called to a man in the distance.

"Johnny! Johnny!" he called in a heavy accent.

A miner walked toward them. Julia recognized the miner. It was Mr. Zarlingo from the boxcars! He came up to Julia. He looked into her eyes.

"Yes, boy, what is it?" asked Mr. Zarlingo.

Maybe he knows I'm a girl, thought Julia. 'What if he won't deliver the note about Papa? Julia considered running away before Mr. Zarlingo blew her cover. Then her whole plan would be a failure. No, Julia had one chance, and she was taking it. She avoided Mr. Zarlingo's eyes and held the note out to him.

Mr. Zarlingo looked at Julia studying her for a moment.

She held her breath.

"You look like someone I know. What's your name?" asked Mr. Zarlingo.

Julia froze. He would recognize her voice if she spoke.

"This boy doesn't understand English," said Mr. Zarlingo after a moment.

Julia started breathing again. Maybe her disguise fooled Mr. Zarlingo. Maybe he recognized her and played along. Maybe Mr. Zarlingo was a spy for the union. Julia realized she would never know the answers to these questions.

Julia watched while he took note and read it.

"Mr. Evans wants Mike Cito back up here," he said. "Thanks, boy. I'll get him." Mr. Zarlingo turned and disappeared into the mine.

Julia waved at the Greek men and jogged back into the woods. She had no idea how long she had been gone, but she knew she had to get back to school quickly. She ran and prayed that her plan would work. Julia hoped that Mr. Parker would not create an accident at all. She hoped she had succeeded in getting Papa out of danger. She hoped that the Parkers' laundry bag and Mama's coat were still where she left them, and she hoped that by another miracle she would get back to school in time, before anyone noticed she had left.

# Lost and Found

J ulia counted her steps as she ran. It calmed her mind. "Five hundred-twelve, five hundred-thirteen, five hundred-fourteen."

She saw light ahead through the trees and she knew she was close to school. She slowed down to a trot and looked around the trees for Mama's coat and the Parkers' laundry. She saw pine trees and aspen but no pile of clothes. They weren't anywhere in sight!

Julia had no way to mark where she left them. She heard children laughing and yelling. Julia knew they were still outside playing, but it would do her no good if she couldn't find Mama's coat and the Parkers' laundry bag.

Julia sped in circles in and out of trees. She was running out of time. She couldn't go back to class dressed as a boy! More seconds slipped by. I have to take a chance and get out of the trees, she thought. It's the only way to get my bearings. Julia ran to the edge of the trees. She peeked out and saw her classmates to the left. She had swung too far right when she returned from the mine. Julia went back into the trees and made her way left. She saw a lump about twenty yards in front of her by a clump of aspen trees.

"There you are," she said to the Parkers' laundry bag. She darted toward it.

Julia tore off Frank's coat and hat. She pulled off Teddy's pants. Julia folded them and carefully placed them back in the Parkers' laundry bag. She brushed the snow off Mama's coat and pulled it on — one sleeve and then the other. She tucked Frank's coat inside her own and stuffed his hat into Mama's pocket. She heard the school bell. Miss Crawford was ringing the signal for everyone to come back in, and Julia was still in the woods!

She ran out of the trees with all the breath she had left in her. The school door closed behind the last student in line. Julia bolted for it. A few moments later she grabbed the handle, swung it open and threw herself inside. Everyone was already sitting down.

"The good thing is that they won't see me hang Frank's coat and hat," said Julia to herself. "The bad thing is that I'm going to be in trouble with Miss Crawford for being late."

Julia moved another student's hat and coat, from the hook where Frank's hung earlier, to an open hook. She put Frank's hat on the hook and then his coat over it. She hung the Parkers' laundry bag and then covered it with Mama's coat.

"Where is Julia Iannacito?" Miss Crawford yelled.

No one spoke.

"I'm back here, Miss Crawford," said Julia.

"You're late. Why aren't you in your seat?" demanded Miss Crawford.

"I'm coming. I'm sorry," said Julia.

"I demand to know where you were," said Miss Crawford.

# Adventure

"**I**'m waiting for an answer. Tell me where you were," said Miss Crawford.

Julia knew everyone was staring at her.

"I...I...I was using the outhouse. My stomach is upset," said Julia.

There were a few chuckles. Julia would have been embarrassed if she had really been in the outhouse, but the fact that she was covering her whereabouts kept her from feeling embarrassed at all.

"Let's hope you can sit through the rest of class," said Miss Crawford.

"Yes, Ma'am," said Julia.

Julia hoped she could sit through the rest of class too. She thought now of Papa. She imagined him getting the message from Mr. Evans. She imagined him walking up out of the mine. She imagined him safe and well.

Miss Crawford wrote math problems on the board. They were ordinary problems on an ordinary afternoon done by ordinary school children. Julia's life hadn't been ordinary since yesterday at about this same time, when she started wishing and Teddy blamed her for his spitball.

Julia worked her division problems. It was relaxing focusing on the numbers. They made sense to her. It still didn't make sense to her that Mr. Parker would want to hurt people on purpose. It didn't make sense to her that mine owners were having their miners shot in Ludlow. It didn't make sense to her that the mine owners wouldn't work with the union to treat the mine workers better.

It wasn't fair. Fairness seemed like a simple thing to Julia. Why was it so hard for the mine owners to do such a simple thing?

The afternoon dragged on slowly. Julia thought of the day she watched a snail crawl around a rock on the bank of the Yampa. It took forever. Miss Crawford seemed to be going through each math problem in slow motion. Finally, she finished explaining the way to solve the last sixth grade problem.

"It's time to get ready to go home," said Miss Crawford. "Teddy, would you ring the bell, please?"

"Sure, Miss Crawford," said Teddy.

He sprang out of his seat and rang the bell loudly. Teddy grabbed his coat and zipped out of the door while the rest of the students were just beginning to pull on their coats.

Julia watched Frank put on his coat and hat. He didn't seem to notice anything different. Julia got into Mama's coat and flung the Parkers' laundry bag over her shoulder.

"How's your stomach, Julia?" asked Frank when they were outside.

"My stomach?" said Julia.

"You were late from recess," said Frank.

"Right. Thanks. I'm much better now," said Julia.

"I'm sorry I couldn't talk with you during recess since I had to help Miss Crawford. What did you want?" asked Frank.

"Oh, I had a question but I figured it out on my own," said Julia.

"Was it about the mine or Ludlow?" whispered Frank.

"I took care of it. I'll see you later," said Julia.

She walked toward home. Everything looked normal outside. The trees never know what happens to people, thought Julia. She headed down the road toward the Parkers' house.

Julia knocked on the back door. Mrs. Parker didn't ask her to come inside today. Julia didn't mind. She would feel strange inside the Parkers' house now. Mrs. Parker took the laundry bag and handed Mama's pay to Julia.

"Thank your mother for me," said Mrs. Parker.

"I sure will," said Julia.

She walked away and headed toward the boxcars. Julia looked at the snow and the trees as she walked. Before she turned onto the road that led to the river, she glanced in the opposite direction.

Julia saw something moving. It looked like a large blob. She squinted her eyes to be sure she wasn't imaging it. The thing was coming down from the road to the right. It was the road that led from the mines.

What could it be? Julia wondered.

Then Julia did something she had never done before. She always went straight home from the Parkers, but today was a day out of the ordinary. Today was filled with adventure, and another one was in front of her. She turned away from the direction of her boxcar, to get a better look at the dark shape. It was coming straight at her.

# The Thing

J ulia decided that the blob looked like a huge black spider with eight wiggling legs. As she got closer, the spider's legs became four, coal-dusted men.

They carried an object between them. After another dozen steps, Julia saw a flat surface with something on it in the middle of the men. Whatever it was, it was covered up.

Julia's heart beat faster. Yesterday she made one little wish for things to be different. Strange things had been happening ever since. With her note delivered to the mines and Papa out of danger, her taste for adventure had returned. This was an exciting event and she was a part of it.

Julia skipped forward. She couldn't wait to solve the mystery.

What are they carrying? wondered Julia. Have they found something valuable at the mines? Maybe there are diamonds in Phippsburg. Maybe we'll all be rich!

Julia ran now, getting closer and closer to the men. She saw their faces. They did not smile.

Julia screeched to a stop and gasped. Although the flat board was covered, Julia recognized the shape on it.

"It's a body," she whispered, "a still body. Only dead bodies get covered up like that."

"Little girl," called one of the men, "go to the school. Tell the teacher to ring the bell for a dead miner."

Julia stared at the man who called to her.

A dead miner! Mr. Parker created an accident anyway today, thought Julia. He killed a union worker! Maybe Phippsburg is going to be the next Ludlow where people get killed because they ask to be treated fairly. It is starting to seem like excitement and bad things go together.

"Run!" yelled another man.

They're giving me a job. It's a big job, thought Julia. These men are asking me to do something important. So, Mr. Teddy Parker, I am somebody special, too! Somebody besides you gets picked to do special things. You always get to ring the school bell. Well, I get to tell Teacher to ring the school bell. Maybe I'll be the one to ring the bell, myself. I have a huge, important job!

"Go, little girl! Go!" ordered another man.

As Julia turned to go, something fell out from under the blanket. It dangled in the air. Julia knew what it was. It was an arm. It was a man's arm. It was a dead man's arm. It wore a red, woolen sweater!

# The Red Sweater

"**R**un!" yelled the first man again.

His voice shocked Julia into motion. She aimed herself toward the school and pumped her legs. She had already run many miles today to the mine and back to school. Her legs grew heavy. She felt like she was plowing through raw macaroni dough.

Julia's thoughts burst into fear over what she had just seen. Her breaths grew short and choppy. It was as if there was no oxygen left in the winter air.

The road back to the school was the same. The pine trees, aspen trees, and snow were the same. The Yampa River where she ran over the bridge was the same, but Julia was not the same.

In her mind all she saw was the arm with the red sweater. Papa's red sweater!

My plan failed! Papa never got my message! He didn't get away from the face in time. He was in the way when Mr. Parker created his make-believe accident. Mr. Parker hurt Papa when he was trying to get rid of a union spy. Maybe Mr. Parker thinks Papa is a spy for the union!

"This can't be happening! Other men at the mine must wear red sweaters. There have to be many red sweaters in Phippsburg," Julia said to herself.

Julia thought back to the trip she took with Mama. Angela was ready to be born. Papa put Mama in the back of a wagon and sent her to Oakcreek. The wagon driver delivered flour, sugar, and coffee from Denver to the mining town grocery stores. Papa told Julia to go along and translate for Mama.

Julia was only six years old, but she already spoke English much better than her parents. She held Mama's hand during the long, bumpy ride.

When they arrived in Oakcreek she helped Mama into the doctor's office. A woman sat at a desk inside.

"The doctor's out on another call," said the woman. Her English was sprinkled with an Irish accent.

Julia told Mama. She saw Mama's face twist at the words.

"Tell her it is time for the baby to come," said Mama. "Tell her I can't wait for the doctor."

Julia told the woman what Mama had said, although it wasn't necessary. The woman knew.

"Tell your mama that I am a midwife. Tell her that I can deliver her baby for only five dollars instead of twelve dollars that the doctor would charge."

Julia translated the message. Mama nodded.

Two hours later, Angela was wrapped in a blanket, and asleep in Mama's arms. Julia paid the midwife and helped Mama walk outside. The wagon driver had finished his deliveries and was putting ropes in the truck.

"Can you take us back to Phippsburg, please?" Julia asked.

"I didn't think you'd be done already," said the man.

"I can see we have three passengers for the ride back."
He nodded toward the bundle in Mama's arms.

Mama looked up and down the street. Julia looked too.

"Is this the first time you've been to Oakcreek?" he asked.

"Yes," said Julia.

Mama stared at a store across the street. She studied the clothes, hanging on display, in the window. Mama put the money left over from paying the midwife instead of the doctor in Julia's hand.

"Go buy your father a sweater, Julia. He gets cold in the mines. Buy that red one in the window. It looks warm."

Julia watched the driver help Mama get into the back of the wagon. Julia walked quickly across the street.

There was so much to see in the store, but Julia didn't have time.

"I want to buy the red sweater in the window," she told the man at the cash register.

A moment later Julia paid him and dashed out of the store with the red sweater wrapped in brown paper and tied with string. Julia was seated next to Mama and baby Angela all in less than five minutes. Julia handed Mama the change. Mama cradled her new baby, and Julia cradled the paper-wrapped sweater all the way back to Phippsburg.

When Papa got home from the mines that night, he had a new daughter and a new sweater.

"How did you pay for the doctor and this sweater?" he asked in Italian.

"We got a bargain today. The doctor was out, so a midwife delivered our baby. It cost less. The sweater will keep you warm," said Mama.

They watched Papa put on his new sweater.

It was the same sweater he wore every day to the mines. It was the same sweater he hung up in the boxcar every night. It was the same sweater Julia saw on the dead man's arm when it swung out from under the blanket!

# The Bell Ringer

"There must be lots of men who wear red sweaters at the mine," said Julia out loud. "Lots of men," she whispered. "It's not my Papa's sweater. It can't be Papa's sweater!"

Julia stumbled up the stone steps of the school and pushed open the wooden door.

"Teacher?" she squeaked. "Miss Crawford!" She tried again.

Julia hardly recognized her own voice.

Julia looked around the empty classroom. Clean tablets sat on desktops, ready for Monday's lessons. The chalkboard was wiped clean. Julia remembered the small oil mark left by the tip of her nose yesterday. She squinted her eyes on the spot where it had been. The room was quiet.

Julia knew what to do. She ran again. Her legs felt like they were filling up with lead as she pushed them toward the large school bell.

Julia grabbed the rope. She pulled the rope with her right hand. The loud tone of the sliver bell vibrated through her head. She pulled the rope again and the second tone vibrated through her chest. She kept pulling the rope. The bell swung faster as it rang, *Ding-ding-dong, Ding-ding-dong.*

Julia rang the bell over and over. Her hands felt numb and her arm grew stiff. She didn't know how long she rang the bell. She was certain she must be deaf from the ringing.

She stopped and leaned against the wooden frame holding the school bell.

"What should I do now?" she asked. "Every day is the same. Every day nothing changes. Every day I know what to do, but now nothing is the same. What do I do now?"

The bell continued ringing, but it was slowing. Julia turned and made her way down the stairs. She felt like her blood was draining out of her. She feared that she was walking down into a hole in her life, and she would never find the way to climb out.

From the bottom of the stairs, the school looked cold and empty to Julia. Cold and empty like it would be without Papa. Julia felt like crying, but her tears were stuck.

Julia looked out into the street. Women and children gathered. Julia saw that some of them were crying, but she couldn't hear them. She heard only bells ringing in her ears.

Julia saw the black spider shape approaching over the top of the crowd. She knew what it was now. The burden of knowing weighted her down worse than twenty winter coats, worse than ten bags of the Parkers' laundry, worse than trying to deliver a hundred notes to the mine disguised as a boy. Julia walked slowly out into the road to look for Mama. How could she tell Mama? What could she say?

# The Apology

J ulia saw fear and dread painted on every face.
A woman spoke to her. Julia watched her lips move,
but couldn't hear what the woman said. The crowd
moved toward the men and the body. Julia recognized
students from school.

"Who is it?" a girl asked.

Julia read the girl's lips. Julia's mouth was dry. She couldn't
speak. Julia could only shake her head.

She saw Teddy, Paulina, and Mrs. Parker running toward
the crowd. They didn't seem as scared as everyone else.
They looked curious, like they were going to a street fight.
Teddy jumped up and down and pulled Mrs. Parker along
by the hand.

Julia recognized a Greek woman from the boxcars and
Mrs. Brunetti. Where is Mama in this mob? she wondered.

The crowd formed a circle around the covered body. Julia
noticed Teddy pushing his way to the front.

Then Julia saw her. There was Mama with some others
from the boxcar houses. Julia walked toward her. Other
people kept walking between them. Mama seemed to get

farther away with each step. Julia saw Lucia and Angela hanging onto Mama's long skirt.

Julia spied a boxcar miner out of the corner of her eye. It was one of the men from Ireland who spoke English. He was walking straight toward Mama!

Oh no! thought Julia. I must be there when he tells her.

It was as if the desire to protect Mama overpowered Julia's own growing ache. Julia walked faster. Mama seemed to only see the miner getting closer to her.

Teddy's sister, Paulina Parker, came out of the crowd and yanked Julia's arm. Julia could barely hear Paulina's voice over the ringing in her own ears.

"I'm sorry about yesterday at school," Paulina said.

"What?" said Julia as if she didn't understand.

"I apologize about saying you made the spitball," said Paulina. "I was sticking up for Teddy."

"Uh-huh," said Julia.

"They say it's your father because of the red sweater," said Paulina.

Julia moved away before she heard the rest of Paulina's sentence. She bolted toward Mama now. Julia almost crashed into the miner as they arrived at the same instant in front of Mama.

# The Interpreter

Mama didn't seem to notice Julia standing there. It was if Julia were transparent, as if Mama were looking through clear water. She looked only at the miner. The color drained from her cheeks. Angela and Lucia clung to her sides like snow on a hill. They were silent, frozen in place. Mama glanced at Julia with tear-filled eyes. She suddenly seemed to recognize her oldest daughter.

"Julia?" Mama asked, as if it was a whole question.

Julia tried to speak, but her lips wouldn't move. She knew somehow this was all her fault. She had wished for excitement. She had wanted something out of the ordinary to happen. She had dreamed of a different life, but not like this!

Julia thought again of how Papa told her that wishes are like fishes. They swim away before you can catch them, before they can do you any good. Julia formed a wish in her heart, caught it and held on. Please let Papa be alive, she wished.

"Something terrible has happened," said the miner.

Julia swallowed. She heard herself translating the man's words for Mama.

Julia felt like she was standing outside of her body, and watching herself speak to her mother.

Mama nodded.

Julia nodded as if to translate. Although she knew it wasn't necessary, she couldn't stop herself from nodding with Mama.

"Mike Cito," said the miner.

Julia kept nodding. Yes, Mike Cito, she thought. I wish he would stop right there and not say anything else. Julia held her breath.

"Mike Cito," said the miner, louder. He raised his eyes and looked beyond Mama.

Oh no, he's going to make a speech to the whole crowd, Julia thought.

"Mike Cito," said Mama. Her voice broke on the "o" and she put her hand to her mouth as if to keep Papa's name from falling out.

The crowd hushed. It parted like a river flowing through melting ice in the springtime. Then Julia looked up and saw them. Dark faces moved through the mass of women and children. A river of coal-dust covered men poured down from the mines and flowed through the middle of the crowd. The black river was coming right at them.

Julia saw the whites of the men's eyes shining on the black backgrounds of their faces. Other men spread into the crowd. They reached out with coal-dust covered hands to hug wives and children. Julia heard low yelps and cries as family members released emotion they had bottled up with their worst fears.

The miner spoke again. "Mike, Mike Cito," he repeated louder.

Why does he keep on saying Papa's name? Why must he keep saying it? Julia wondered.

The miner waved his arms. This man has gone mad, thought Julia.

Mama squinted at the miner as if he were a bright sun hurting her eyes.

Julia was barely aware of movement behind her mother. In an instant, a black face appeared. Julia looked over Mama's shoulder into a miner's eyes.

"My note," whispered Julia to herself, "Papa, what happened to my note?"

I want everything back the way it was yesterday before Teddy made me take his punishment, before there was a note from Mr. Parker in my shoe, before I tried to change things, before now, thought Julia.

I know it was Papa's red sweater on the dead man's arm. I saw it with my own eyes. I got my wish for something exciting to happen. This is all my fault!

Julia watched Mama turn and scream into the man's chest. Angela and Lucia spun as they hung onto Mama's legs. What a mistake, a terrible mistake, thought Julia. She held her breath. Then everything started turning. The sky and the ground traded places.

Julia felt herself falling, drifting, and then it was dark and silent.

# The Revelation

"Julia. Julia," a man's voice called Julia through her dream. It sounded far away like it was coming from down the road.

"Julia!" she heard again.

Julia opened her eyes and saw blurry human shapes around her. Mama's face came into focus. She knew the smaller forms were Lucia and Angela. In a moment she could see them. Julia closed her eyes again. She did not want to wake up into a world without Papa.

Angela said, "You fainted, Julia. Open your eyes."

Julia did not want to scare her little sister. She opened her eyes into slits.

Julia made out a dark face behind Mama.

It looks like Mr. Zarlingo from the boxcars or another miner, Julia thought.

"Julia," said the man.

She knew the voice like she knew her own hand.

"Papa?" asked Julia opening her eyes wide to bring the image into focus.

"Julia, wake up, Julia," he said.

Julia sat up. Her eyes cleared. A sob caught in her throat. Papa bent down and reached for her. Papa was here! He was alive! Julia wrapped her arms around Papa's neck and pushed her face into his rough cheek. His whiskers pinched her skin. It made him seem more real to her. Maybe Julia's note had helped Papa after all. Julia sat back and looked at her father. A tear escaped, and Julia brushed it away so Papa wouldn't see. She noticed that Papa wore only his two cotton shirts.

"Where is your red sweater?" asked Julia.

People gathered around Julia's family now. They pushed in closer to see what was happening.

"That is the sad story," said Papa, speaking carefully. "I let someone else wear my sweater for a while today. It was someone who didn't go down into the mines very often. It was someone who had such a nice white shirt. I lent him my sweater so he wouldn't get his good clothes covered with coal dust."

Papa lifted Julia to her feet. She held onto his arms to steady herself.

"Who is it, Mike?" asked the miner who came to talk to Mama. "I thought it was you. We all thought it was you."

"Who is it?" asked another miner.

Papa put his fingers to his lips and shook his head. Julia saw many faces pointed at Papa and then turn toward the four miners and the dead man. People walked away from Julia's family. Miners, women, and children moved like they were metal shavings being pulled by a huge magnet toward the blanketed body.

Julia's family blended into the crowd and became part of the circle surrounding the four men and the covered body.

The four miners who had carried the body, the miners who had carefully placed it on the ground, the miners who had been standing guard around it, protecting it, backed away and became part of the noiseless crowd.

An older miner walked up to the body. He took hold of the blanket that concealed it. He pulled back the blanket and revealed the face of the man who wore Papa's red sweater.

Julia's gasp was swallowed up in sea of groans from the crowd.

"Father! Father!" someone screamed hoarsely.

Julia recognized the voice before she saw who was yelling.

# The Miners

J ulia saw Teddy throw himself on top of the dead
man. She watched a group of miners move toward
the hysterical boy. It took three strong men to pull
him off of his father's body. Teddy's blue coat was
dotted with blood. A patch of dark red blood remained on
Mr. Parker's temple. Mrs. Parker and Paulina were engulfed
by a circle of miners' wives. The four miners lifted Mr. Parker's
body and carried it toward the yellow house.

Mr. Evans ran up. Julia recognized him from his picture
in the store. He shook his head back and forth, back and forth
like it was loose. He found Mrs. Evans and they followed
behind the body.

A new fear rippled through the crowd.

A man's voice rang out, "We will keep our shifts at the mine."

"Without Parker, who will know the difference?" called
a voice.

"Show for your shift to keep your job!" ordered the
speaker. "It's almost six o'clock. The night shift starts in
a few minutes. The mine owner will send a new boss.
We don't want trouble in Phippsburg!"

"Not like Ludlow," said a another voice.

"Never like Ludlow!" said the speaker. "If it wasn't for Ludlow, Mr. Parker would be alive right now."

The crowd was still.

Julia searched the miners' faces for a clue. What had happened? What was going on? She saw Frank O'Malley standing with a man and a woman. It must be his father and mother, thought Julia. The man looked like all of the other fathers, covered with coal dust except for his eyes and a lock of yellow hair peeking out from under his cap.

"Never like Ludlow!" repeated a miner.

"Never!" called two more.

"Never!" rang out each miner's voice over the heads of every stunned woman and child.

Papa turned Mama toward the Yampa River and the boxcars. He picked up Angela with one arm and Lucia with the other.

Julia put her hand in her pocket. Mama's payment from Mrs. Parker for doing the laundry was still there.

The crowd shuffled. Day shift miners and their families walked home. Night shift miners walked toward the mine.

The yellow haired father spoke to Frank O'Malley. Julia watched her schoolmate take his mother's arm and walk away.

Julia knew instinctively not to talk. She put her finger to her lips signaling silence to her sisters in Papa's arms, but it wasn't necessary. The other boxcar families walked behind the Citos. Julia looked over her shoulder and met the eyes of the yellow haired miner. He didn't live in the boxcars, but he walked with a man in the group like he was going home, too.

One of the miners called to Papa, "Mike, why did Mr. Parker go down into the mine?"

"He was looking for someone," said Papa.

The miner ran to catch up with Papa.

"Who would be so important that Mr. Parker would risk going into the mine?" asked the miner.

"I didn't know the man," said Papa. "I was working in the mine when somebody came down and told me that there was a note from Mr. Evans saying I was supposed to go up and load coal at the top. I was up there shoveling coal when Mr. Parker arrived. He said someone told him there was a union man in the mine talking to miners. Someone said the union man was working close to the face where they were cutting fresh coal."

"That explains it. He was going after a union man," said the miner.

"I don't think there was a union man in our mine," said Papa, "but poor Mr. Parker was standing in the way when that rock hit him in the head. It hit him just right."

"It was for nothing if there wasn't a union man in the mine," said the miner.

"It was for nothing," said Papa.

Julia looked back at Frank O'Malley's father. Why was he walking with the boxcar families? He looked ahead as if he was going somewhere past the boxcars, but Julia felt certain he was listening to every word Papa and the other miner were saying. Then she saw it. It was slight, but Julia was sure. The yellow haired man put something into another miner's hand. It was something small like money, or a key, or a note, or a rock.

# The Wish

What had Frank's father passed to the other miner? Frank O'Malley had said that his father did everything Boss Parker wanted. Now Julia wondered if he was a union man. He looks like every other miner, thought Julia. Maybe he's spying now. Maybe he wants to hear everything that Papa knows about the accident.

"I told Mr. Parker not to go down any further," said Papa. "I told him it was dangerous, but he was going anyway. It was to look out after his mine, he said. That's when I told him to wear my sweater to protect his nice clothes. I told him to be careful since he wasn't used to going down into the mine."

"You're a good man, Mike," said the miner. "You were a good worker for Mr. Parker. I'll see you in the coal tomorrow."

"Good-bye," said Papa.

Julia watched the yellow haired man stroll away. Papa slid open the heavy door of their boxcar home.

"Here is your money for the laundry from Mrs. Parker, Mama," said Julia.

"Thank you, Julia. Poor Mrs. Parker. What will she do now? It's so sad. I baked bread early this morning. Take this loaf to Mrs. Parker," said Mama.

Julia winced at the thought of going into the yellow house, but she obeyed Mama. She looked at Papa as if to take a photograph of him with her eyes. Julia picked up the loaf of Mama's bread and walked back outside. Night covered Phippsburg.

Although Julia's legs felt shaky, she aimed them toward the Parkers' yellow house. She knew the way in the dark. She didn't mind walking now. Julia needed a little time to get over all that had taken place. She thought about her silent wish to have something exciting happen for a change. She thought about Mr. Parker's note and Ludlow. She thought about writing her own note and running through the trees dressed as a boy. She remembered worrying all day about Papa getting away from the face and then seeing the arm in the red sweater.

When Julia got close to the yellow house, she stopped for a moment. She had felt the thrill of adventure, the specialness of being important, the horror of being terrified, and the relief of being saved from unbearable grief. She had felt the excitement of having things out of the ordinary happen, and she didn't like it. She closed her eyes and wished to have her plain life back again. She blinked three times for good luck.

She walked the last few steps to the yellow house. Julia realized that Mr. Parker would never come home to this house again. He would never be the boss of the mine again. Julia hoped that the new boss would be kinder, more fair, and make things better at the mine. Julia took a breath and knocked on the Parkers' kitchen door.

# The Visit

The Parkers' back door swung open, and Julia stood face to face with Mrs. Evans.

"What do you want?" Mrs. Evans asked. Her eyes were dull. "This is no time for a visit."

"Mama wanted Mrs. Parker to have this loaf of bread. She baked it fresh today," said Julia. She held the bread out to Mrs. Evans.

"I'll give it to Mrs. Parker," said Mrs. Evans.

Behind Mrs. Evans through the kitchen, Julia saw Mrs. Parker sitting with Mr. Evans and some other people.

"Who is it?" asked Mrs. Parker.

"It's Julia Iannacito with a loaf of bread from her Mama," answered Mrs. Evans.

"Tell her to wait a minute," said Mrs. Parker. "Don't let her leave."

Mrs. Parker's voice sounded funny to Julia, like Mrs. Parker was talking but she wasn't really inside of her body.

Mrs. Evans closed the door to keep the cold out, or in; Julia wasn't sure which was icier. She looked at the cloudy puffs her breath made in the night air. She counted forty-seven puffs. The door opened again. Teddy appeared behind Mrs. Evans.

"This belongs to your father. My mom says to give it back to him," said Teddy, thrusting the red sweater at Julia.

Julia looked at Teddy's swollen face and sunken, red eyes. She guessed that if Teddy could trade places with her, he would. Teddy would want to live in the boxcar where a papa would be coming home for dinner tonight, instead of in the yellow house where there would be no father tonight or ever again. Teddy would trade. Julia would never want to trade with Teddy again. She knew now how lucky she was.

"Thank you, Teddy," she said.

Teddy stared blankly at Julia, or through her like she was a ghost, or like she was not there at all. He walked away. Mrs. Evans closed the door without saying another word.

Julia was glad she hadn't said a mean thing to Teddy yesterday after he blamed her for the spitball. It really wouldn't have helped anything, and it would have made Julia feel terrible. All of the meanness in the world just happened to Teddy Parker when that rock hit his father in the head. No one could be meaner than that!

# The Boxcar House

J ulia walked back home cradling Papa's red sweater. She held it close to her chest as she had all the way home from Oakcreek in the back of a truck so many years before. Phippsburg was frozen solid now, but Julia did not feel cold. She felt warm inside and lucky, lucky to have a warm place to live, and lucky to have Papa alive.

When Julia slid open the door and walked into the box-car, heat from the stove hit her face. The room smelled like noodles and tomato sauce. Julia hung up Mama's coat.

"Julia's home," said Papa. "Put the macaroni on the table, Mama, and let's eat!"

Julia handed the red sweater to Papa. She touched his arm.

Papa took his red sweater and hung it next to Mama's coat.

"It's okay now, Julia," he said. "Someday I will get a good job with the railroad, and we will live in a real house instead of a boxcar."

"I like our house, Papa," said Julia.

Julia thought of the yellow house and Teddy. She thought of the newspaper headlines about Ludlow and the miners' union. She thought about Frank O'Malley's yellow-haired father and how he followed them and handed something to another miner. Julia knew there was a puzzle to put together. She knew it was a mystery to solve like a math problem where everything falls into place and points to the right answer. She knew she had enough pieces to put most of the puzzle together. But Julia buried her thoughts deep into her mind like coal in a mine. She could dig them out tonight, tomorrow, or never.

"I like things the way they are," Julia said.

She helped Mama put food on the table. They all sat in the middle of their boxcar at the table. Julia, Mama, Angela, and Lucia folded their hands and closed their eyes. Papa began the evening prayer.

"We give thanks for our lives, our family, this food, and this great country where dreams come true," said Papa.

"And where wishes come true, too," added Julia in her mind.

"Amen," said everyone together.

"Let's eat," said Papa.

Julia took a bite. The macaroni, made with Mama's hands and Julia's help, tasted better than ever.

"We are very lucky," said Mama.

"We are very lucky," agreed Julia. She knew that she had everything in the world she needed right there inside that warm boxcar.

# The History
# Behind
# the Story

Primary and secondary sources which
tie in with the story you just read.

# Family History

O*ut of the Ordinary* by Michelle M. Barone is historical fiction. Much of what is described in the book actually took place in the early part of the 20th century. In fact, Julia is the grandmother of the author, who based the story on the accounts she heard so often from her grandmother. Of course, the details in the dialogue and some of the descriptions of other characters in the story are fictionalized. That is, they are based on the truth, but changed slightly or sometimes even totally made up by the author.

In this section of the book, several primary source documents and graphics are presented. You can read and look over some of the records from that period in our nation's history and from the personal family history of Julia.

Primary sources are written documents, graphics, or oral histories that were recorded by someone who was involved in the event or an eyewitness to it. Very often authors use these kind of documents to create their stories and to back up their work with factual information. Sometimes the written documents appeared as newspaper accounts, journal entries, or letters, to name a few. We've included a letter from Julia, our heroine in the story, which she wrote for readers at the age of 94.

To all Students

As I write this letter to you I am 94 years old. Since I was your age I've seen many changes in my life, such as the automobile, airplanes, T.V. computers, washing machines, dish washers, wireless phones & many more. You will see many changes in your life too, but some things always remain the same. Get a good education learn all you can. I say knowledge is like money in the bank, the more you put in the more you will have to use when you need it.

Read & learn all you can.

Julia

8-14-04

*Left to right*: Adeline, Julia, Clementine (Mama), Angeline, Mike Cito (Papa)

*Left to right*: Michelle (the author), Julia today, and Alex, the author's daughter

# The Ludlow Massacre

Coal mining was hard and dangerous work. Many miners were hurt or killed in the mines. In 1913, some Colorado coal miners joined together in a union to ask the mine owners for improvements. Miners wanted a raise in pay from $1.68 a day. They wanted eight hour shifts and to be paid for all of their work, including cleaning up around the mines. Miners wanted to be able to shop anywhere, not just at stores owned by the mine where prices were high. They also wanted Colorado mining laws to be followed and no company guards in the mines.

Powerful mine owners like the Rockfellers had other ideas. They kept miners from joining unions by beating them, tarring and feathering them, or leaving them out in the prairie wilderness to survive alone.

On September 13, 1913, eleven thousand miners began to strike. The mine owners kicked them and their families out of company owned houses and brought immigrants into the country to work the mines. The striking miners and their families lived through the cold winter in tents. Mine guards shot at the tents. Even members of the National Guard were paid by the mine owners to take their side against the miners.

On April 20, 1914, guards set off three bombs in the tent camp near Ludlow. The guards also starting shooting. Many people were killed. The news spread all over the country.

There was a protest at the Denver Capital demanding that the National Guard in Ludlow be tried for murder. Demonstrators picketed at the Rockfeller office in New York City. President Woodrow Wilson sent federal troops to get things under control.

Today, Ludlow is a symbol for the struggle of workers to organize in the United States. There is a monument in Ludlow, Colorado honoring the people who gave their lives in the fight for human rights and better working conditions.

*Monument to those who died in The Ludlow Massacre* Photo by Joanna Sampson

In the text of this book, on pages 42 to 43, the author has quoted a newspaper article from *The Rocky Mountain News* of April 21,1914.  In the story, Julia reads some of the article while waiting for Mrs. Evans to get groceries.  Here is what the actual article looked like:

Here is a cartoon that appeared in the newspaper, *The Denver Post*, on April 23, 1914.

# Going to School in a One-Room Schoolhouse

*Vanishing One-Room Rural Schools*
by Leo VanMeer

Only an occasional one-room rural school remains in use today. At the beginning of the twentieth century, about the time when I was born, more than a thousand provided educational opportunities in the nation's rural areas.

A parade of mental pictures bring into sharp focus my formative years when life, at one time, centered around a rural school and our family farm.

Fondly I recall the many times a clanging school bell called pupils to classes. I can still hear the bell sound begin with a hesitant ding dong, rising in crescendo to send a vital message across fertile farm lands. After additional bell rope tugs, the action slowed, then ceased, and the bell sound retreated into silence.

Each day, with school in session, I joined other pupils, clutching a lunch pail and assorted books. Together we trudged along a dirt or snow-covered road to a common destination. On the way, we learned to know each other better and how to get along together. No busses, automobiles, or fond parents driving a horse-drawn vehicle transported us to school. We walked, benefitted by exercise.

Rural school teachers, with minimal training, imparted

knowledge with love and understanding. We may have learned by attrition and repetition, as someone may suggest; but a number of my classmates graduated from the local high school, sometimes with honors, and attended college or a university. Some graduates became leaders in their chosen field.

Anyone who might be expecting a classroom pin-dropping atmosphere would have considered our activity pandemonium. Someone, or so it seemed, was in motion at all times. Yet we learned concentration, a valuable ability to use during later years.

A schoolhouse with more than forty pupils, ranging in grades from one through eight, as well as kindergarten, prompted us to pay little attention to schoolroom activity. Classes passing at frequent intervals, and monitors tending to their respective duties, added little to the disruptive atmosphere. Despite ensuing activity, our work studies proceeded in an orderly fashion. While listening surreptitiously to class recitation, we reviewed each grade, year after year.

The school building, where at one time I attended classes, still remains at the present time. While visiting there recently, I learned the building has been remodeled for a township meeting hall. A dusty, country road, running past the one-time school building and playgrounds, has been replaced by a two-lane paved highway, alive with trucks and automobiles. Horse-drawn vehicles, common during my formative years, are no longer seen today. Vanished years, spent within the aged, sturdy structure, brought back poignant memories.

If you have questions or comments about this article, please e-mail: **leo@vanmeer.com** or write to Leo VanMeer, P.O. Box 8127, Clearwater, FL 33758.

# Letter from a Former Student and Teacher of One-Room Schoolhouses

This letter, by Mrs. Reppie Smith of Sapulpa, Oklahoma, was written to the author of the book, *One-Room Schoolhouses of Arkansas as Seen Through a Pinhole*, by Thomas Harding, 1993.

Memories of my education in a one-room schoolhouse are very many and dear to me. And I do remember most everything. I started at age six in 1914 and finished the eight-grade in 1922. First through eighth grades were taught to about thirty or more students.

The school was Liberty in a little town called Woolsey now. When I was growing up it was called Pitkin. The first graders started to learn their ABCs and numbers from a large chart. Later we received our first book: *The Primer*. From there we were learning words and some arithmetic. Reading, writing, arithmetic, history, spelling, grammar, geography, and penmanship were taught. Of course, the names of some of these subjects have been changed. Spelling and ciphering contests were usually held after the last recess on Fridays.

I don't remember us ever taking school work home to study at night. Coal oil lamps didn't give out much light to study by.

If our teachers had problems teaching that many children in a one-room space with all our different lessons, we didn't know anything about them. If we weren't reciting, we were busy getting our next lesson.

Our heating system was a wood burning stove. Later it was replaced with an upright heater. It was located at the back of the room in the corner.

If I remember right, it was the teacher's job to start the fire when they arrived at the schoolhouse much earlier than time for the children. Older boys brought in wood through the day and they kept the fire going. Our air conditioner was open windows. There were lots of windows and you sure could tell this come winter time.

The water we had to drink came from a hand-dug well. The well was on school property. Water was drawn up by bucket, rope, and pulley. Everyone had their own drinking cups. Some were tin and some were the folding kind. If you had a folding cup, you felt rich. The bucket of water was set on a shelf at the back. Older children kept the water ready for the rest of us.

We had a cloak room for coats, hats, and scarves. A shelf in this little room held our lunches (lard or syrup buckets).

Now, about our rest room. It sat out back. It was nice and roomy. It was much nicer than I had at home. It had three seats you could rest on.

# Photographs and Artifacts

Photographs and artifacts (like a McGuffey's Reader) can also be primary sources. In each of the pictures shown, there is a link to the author's story.

*Children at recess, Milton, ND 1913*

*Interior of Buford School, Marion County, Arkansas. The school was built in 1889.* Courtesy of the Thomas Harding family

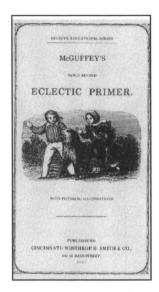

*Cover from a*
McGuffey's Reader

*Spelling lessons from*
*a* McGuffey's Reader

# Acknowledgments

I owe my sincere gratitude to the following people for the part they played in the making of this book:

I thank my beautiful grandmother for telling me her stories over and over, for suggesting ideas and giving me her blessing as I fictionalized parts of the book, and for believing in me always.

I thank Cynthia Camp and Sheryl Connet for their support, encouragement, and patience as I chase another dream, and for hours of listening to me talk about writing.

Thanks to Barbara Boyd for reminding me to never give up, and to Paula Bennett for proofing.

A huge thank you to JoAnne Deitch for her passion for history and enthusiasm for this book. Her expertise and thoughtful suggestions have been invaluable to this project.

Special thanks to Aunt Jody Musso and Uncle Frank Barone for their help plowing through family photographs.

Many thanks to Damian Griffin and Barb Wagers for their technical support on the computer.

Thanks to Jim Kroll and the staff in the Western History wing of the Denver Public Library for their help with the microfiche machine to copy the *Denver Post* and *Rocky Mountain News* articles.

Thank you to Dennis Durkin at the Ross Cherry Creek branch of the Denver Public Library for digging up books to help with my research.

Final thanks to Lisa Wroble at the Institute of Children's Literature for her help as I took this project from a short story to a book, and to Adriane Frye at Henry Holt and Company for her suggestions.